THE GREATES

The Greatest Store in the World

Alex Shearer

Hodder
Children's
Books

a division of Hodder Headline plc

A Catalogue record for this book is available from
the British Library

ISBN 0 340 74336 0

Typeset by Avon Dataset Ltd, Bidford-on-Avon, Warks

Printed and bound in Great Britain by
Clays Ltd, St Ives plc

Hodder Children's Books
A Division of Hodder Headline plc
338 Euston Road
London NW1 3BH

THE GREATEST STORE IN THE WORLD

But I'm too old to be taken in like that. I don't say I can't be taken in at all, but I can't be taken in that way. So I knew as soon as Mum mentioned the game of Hide Under the Bed just what she was up to. I knew now why she'd packed the big suitcase. I knew why we'd come to Scottley's at almost six o'clock on a Saturday night, just when they were about to close. Oh yes, I knew why we were hiding under the big four-poster in the Bedding Department all right, me and Mum, with little Angeline sandwiched between us trying not to sneeze or snort or laugh or giggle. We were moving in. Yes, that's what we were doing. We had come to live at Scottley's, the greatest department store in the world.

CHAPTER ONE

STATEMENT GIVEN TO POLICE SERGEANT
VERONICA CLARKE BY OLIVIA WILLIAMS, IN
THE PRESENCE OF SOCIAL WORKER MRS
PATRICIA DOMINICS AND WOMAN POLICE
OFFICER CHRISTINE MATHLEY.

OLIVIA:

It was our mum said to do it. We were up on the
third floor it must have been, round about closing
time – which I thought was a bit of a funny time to
go shopping for a bed. But she said we needed
one in a desperate hurry and we'd be sure to get
one at Scottley's as they had loads round there.
Hundreds of them – well, dozens anyway – all set
up in lines, just like it was a great big dormitory of
double beds, just like you see on the telly in these
films about places like boarding schools and army
barracks and that.

So I thought it was a bit funny to start with. Because not only were we going shopping for a bed at quarter to six in the evening – which doesn't really give you much time to choose one – we were going to *Scottley's* as well. Which seemed a bit strange to me. In fact it was just as I said to Angeline –

INTERRUPTION BY SERGEANT CLARKE

SERGEANT CLARKE:

Olivia, can you tell us who Angeline is, please? Just for the sake of the record?

OLIVIA:

Yes. She's my little sister. But you already know that as you've met her and she's in the next room with my mum, playing with that thing you gave her. So why are you asking?

SERGEANT CLARKE:

It's just for the statement, that's all. To make it clear.

OLIVIA:

Oh, right. Here – are you recording all this?'

SERGEANT CLARKE:

Yes, we are. Why? Does it put you off?

OLIVIA:

Me? No. I don't mind. Shall I go on then?

SERGEANT CLARKE:

Please.

OLIVIA:

Right. Well, as I said to Angeline, I thought it was peculiar for a couple of reasons. But I didn't say anything to our mum. Not straightaway. Not with all the problems she'd been having and with us having to get out of the flat. And what with Dad being away too and no one really knowing quite when he was coming back from his job on the oil rig. It was all rather difficult.

Anyway, I didn't like to bother Mum, but it did make me wonder. I mean you don't go shopping for a *bed*, do you, not at a quarter to six on a Saturday night, not when you've only got a few minutes before the shop closes. I mean, it's a pint of milk or a loaf of bread, that's more the kind of stuff you rush out to buy when you've only got fifteen minutes to spare before the shop closes. Not a *bed*. Because a bed's a big thing, isn't it? And you always take your time to buy big things. It's *little* things you buy in a hurry. Unless it's jewellery, of course, which is very expensive, even if it is little. You wouldn't buy that in a hurry, you'd take your time choosing it. Not that it ever bothered us. We never bought any jewellery anyway.

So that was the first thing I thought was odd.

And the next thing I thought was peculiar – as I might have said already – was what were we doing in *Scottley's*? Because, I mean, I don't know if you've ever been in Scottley's – oh, you have, right. Then you'll know what I'm talking about. Because Scottley's is the most fantastic shop in town. Probably even in the whole *world*. Not that I've actually seen the whole world, but that's what I'd imagine.

Scottley's is so big it's almost like a town, all on its own. And I think they must sell everything there. Really, I do think they must. Absolutely *everything*. And I bet that if they don't sell it in Scottley's it just doesn't exist. And their Toy Department alone . . . have you been up there? Well, their Toy Department is just absolutely enormous. It goes on and on forever. And just when you think it's about to stop, you turn a corner and discover another bit. And they sell food and drinks and everything in Scottley's. Not in the Toy Department, mind, but there's restaurants and cafés everywhere. But it's the best department store in the whole world, it really is.

But I'll tell you something. It may be the best, but it definitely is not the cheapest. No way. It's all the rich people who shop at Scottley's and we never do. We just go in there for a warm-up, because it's always like toast in Scottley's, except in the summer, when they keep it nice and cool. So that's what we used to do. In the winter we'd go in for a warm-up, and in the summer we'd go in for a cool-down. And in the springtime we'd go in to get out of the rain. And in the autumn . . . well, I can't remember what the autumn reason for going in there was, but we'd go in anyway, just for the heck of it.

But we never bought anything. Never. Not so much as a pencil. We couldn't afford it. For the cost of a pencil in Scottley's, you could have bought five ordinary pencils anywhere else. Not that I'm saying they were crooks in Scottley's, mind, or that they were out to overcharge you. I'm sure their pencils were five times better than anyone else's and they lasted six times as long. And they probably *had* to charge you more anyway because it must cost a lot of money to keep a place like that open, what with all the lights and the window displays and all the people working there, it must cost an absolute fortune.

And those window displays! Have you ever seen them? Yeah! And the ones at Christmas? Yeah! Aren't they amazing? They are, aren't they? I mean, they're like a present in itself.

In fact, one Christmas it was the only present me and Angeline got. Yes. Straight up. No, I'm not kidding. It was that Christmas when Mum said Dad had gone to join the French Foreign Legion . . . or maybe he'd gone exploring in South America. Anyway, it was one or the other, and this big Christmas cheque that he was going to send us to buy presents with, well, it was terrible really, because Mum said he *must* have sent it, but then it went and got lost in the post. So we had no money for Christmas – not for so much as a feather, never mind a turkey. Not that I'd have eaten a turkey anyway, because I don't much like the thought of eating turkeys myself. I'd probably rather have had a pizza.

Anyway, Mum was a bit upset about it at first, and you could tell she was dreading telling us, but she had to in the end and she said, 'Girls, I'm afraid there's some bad news this year. Your dad's cheque that he must have sent for Christmas has gone and got lost in the post. So I'm afraid there aren't going to be any presents this year, none at all. I'm sorry.'

So we were upset too, to start with, but maybe not as much as she'd expected, and we soon cheered up when she said, 'I'll tell you what! I'll tell you what we can do for a special treat! We can go and see the Christmas window display at Scottley's. Because that costs nothing – except for the effort of getting there – and we can walk it in fifteen minutes and then we'll have a hot cocoa when we get back.'

And that was what we did. And I tell you, those window displays at Scottley's, they really *made* Christmas, what with the crib and the stars and the reindeer and the tinsel and the tree, and that window with a whole rooftop in it, with Santa Claus's legs sticking out of the chimney. Well, it was unbelievable.

It wasn't quite the same as getting a *real* present, of course, but it was the next best thing. We used to dream sometimes of getting a present from Scottley's Toy Department. But we never did. All we ever got was to go and to look, and looking was our present. And they couldn't stop us from going into Scottley's and *looking*, could they? Because how would they know that we weren't rich millionaires who had just won the National Lottery and who had come in to buy the whole place up? That's what my mum said anyway, and I'm sure she was right.

I tell you what though, there was a man who stood at the front door there, right at Scottley's main entrance, and he had the smartest uniform and the biggest whiskers you had ever seen. They were huge, just like he'd pinched them off a walrus when it wasn't looking. Our mum said it was called a handlebar moustache, because his whiskers were as wide and as long as the handlebars on a bike. And they were too.

And you should have seen his uniform – well, you probably *have* seen it – it was the fanciest uniform you could ever imagine. It had gold braid and medals everywhere and curly bits on the shoulders and around the cuffs. And to top it off he were these dainty white gloves, which looked a bit odd, in a way, on a man with a big moustache like his. But yes, he had these little white gloves that actually buttoned up at the wrist. Amazing. And his trousers had gold stripes running down the outsides, and he had such sharp creases on his trousers that you could have chopped up onions with them – if he'd been willing to lend them to you. But I don't think he would. He didn't look like the sort of man who'd be kind enough to let you borrow his trousers for chopping up onions.

He had amazingly shiny shoes too, even when

it was muddy and rainy outside. So they must have been special ones that he changed into when he got to work. And on top of the amazing trousers, he also had this amazing tail coat. And on his head he had a pale grey top hat, with even more gold braid around it, which made him look like a walrus with a hat on.

And we nicknamed him Mr Whiskers.

Now his job seemed to involve holding the door open mostly – not that he ever really held it open for *us*. I think he seemed to know, just from looking at us, that we didn't have any money to spend and that we were only going into Scottley's for a warm-up or a cool-down or a bit of a look around.

To be honest, I don't think he would have let us in at all, if it had been left up to him. That or he'd have chucked us out. He used to follow us with his eyes, like we'd come in to pinch things, like we were a gang of shoplifters or something, which we weren't at all. Because my mum is dead honest and she brought us up to be dead honest too. And she'd never steal *anything* from *anybody*, not unless she was really, *really* desperate, like if she was at her wits' end or saw that we were starving hungry or freezing cold. And to tell the truth, I think that *anybody* could get a bit dishonest

9

then. Because it doesn't seem right to me, see, that some people have got so many blankets in their wardrobes that they can't even use them all, no matter how cold it gets, while other people are turning into ice cubes.

But my mum's a really honest person, anyway, that's all I'm saying. And if she's done something bad – and I'm not saying she *did* do anything bad – well, I'm sure it was only because she was desperate and didn't know what else to do. And she'd only have done it for our sakes. She wouldn't do anything like that for herself.

Now this man at the main entrance of Scottley's, as well as holding the door open for people, he also used to sometimes help them carry their shopping to their cars, or he'd maybe go out and whistle up a taxi for them. And for all that he wasn't very welcoming to us, he did have the most tremendous whistle. It was a brilliant whistle, the one he had, and he used to make it by putting two fingers into his mouth and blowing as hard as he could. And the sound he made was so piercing that not only would he whistle up a taxi, he'd stop all the traffic in the street sometimes, as they maybe thought that it was a police car or an ambulance or a fire engine coming by.

Another thing he used to do was tip his hat. But he only did this to rich-looking people and to ladies with big handbags.

'Good morning, modom,' he'd say. 'Lovely morning this morning. Can I open the door for you there, modom? My pleasure. No trouble at all.'

Then he'd tip his hat as he held the door open, and the person would feel ever so swanky. And everyone would look at them and think, 'Who *is* that? They must be someone *very* important.'

But they weren't, not necessarily. Maybe all they were was rich, which doesn't really make you important, not to me anyway. It just makes you rich, that's all. Which must be very nice, I'm sure. But it's not important, not really.

When people were leaving, Mr Whiskers would tip his hat again and he'd help them into a taxi. And they would drop some coins – or sometimes even a note – into his hand, and he'd sneak a look at how much they'd given him and then slip the money into his pocket.

But he never tipped his hat to us. And we never gave him any money. We just used stare at his whiskers and try not to giggle.

After a while, my mum stopped using the front door and we started to go in by one of the side entrances instead, in order to avoid him. Because instead of making us feel welcome, he just made us feel uncomfortable, like we had no business being there, as if we didn't belong in this wonderful store, as if we ought to go round the second-hand shops instead . . .

CHAPTER TWO

So there we were, anyway, shopping for a new bed, last thing on a Saturday night. And I thought it was dead peculiar really, because as far as I could see the very last thing we needed was a new bed. Let alone a new double one. Let alone an *expensive* new double one from Scottley's. Let alone at a quarter to six on a Saturday evening. I said as much to Mum – though there wasn't much point in saying it to little Angeline. She's a bit like a pram, she is, she'll go where she's pushed, and then she'll stay there until you push her somewhere else. Not that I mean she's on wheels. She's not in a wheelchair or anything like that. She just doesn't seem to question things much, or to bother where she is. Just as long as I'm there and Mum's there, she's perfectly happy most of the time. I mean, if you took her on to a bus and said, 'Angeline, we're living on the bus now,' she'd probably just say, 'Righto,' and she'd make a little corner for herself and go round and say hello to everyone and that would be it. She doesn't care where she is, really, just as long as we're all together.

Anyway, I thought it was so peculiar, us going off to buy this bed, that I did say to Mum, 'Mum, do you really think we ought to be doing this?'

And Mum said, 'What do you mean?'

And I said, 'You know, coming to Scottley's to buy a bed?'

And she said, 'Why not? Why shouldn't we come into Scottley's to buy a bed? We're as good as anyone aren't we?'

So I tried a different approach, as I could see she was getting irritated, and I said, 'Yes, Mum, of course we're as good as anyone. We just haven't got as much money as anyone. And I'm just a bit worried, that's all.'

Well, you can say what you like about our mum – and I'm not saying she's perfect, she's got her faults, same as we all have – but one thing about her is that if you ever say you're worried about something, she *listens* to you. She doesn't go, 'Pooh, pooh, that's nothing to bother about,' like some people do. So when I said that I was

14

worried, she paid some attention.

'What is it Livvy?' she said. 'What are you worried about?'

'You, Mum,' I told her, 'going spending all this money that I'm sure you haven't really got on a new big double bed. And from Scottley's, of all places. I mean, why Scottley's, Mum? What's wrong with the Salvation Army shop like we usually go to when we need anything? And why a double bed? Who are you going to share it with when Dad's away on the oil wells and no one knows when he'll be coming back.'

'It's a surprise for him,' Mum explained. But I didn't really believe her and I don't really think she expected me to.

'But why Scottley's, Mum? Why *Scottley's*?'

'Because Scottley's is the best. You can't beat Scottley's for quality. And if you have to liv— that is, if you have to buy a new bed from somewhere, Scottley's is the place.'

We were already in the Bedding Department by then. It wasn't that busy as it was nearing the end of the day and the big Saturday rush was over. The assistant didn't look very pleased to see us either, like she'd hoped it was all over and no more customers would come in, and she could have a quiet fifteen minutes to herself before they shut up the shop.

She looked a bit unhappy about little Angeline too, because the moment we entered the Bedding and Bedroom Furniture Department, Angeline made a bee-line for the biggest bed in the place, kicked off her shoes (because she's got manners) jumped on to the mattress and started bouncing up and down on it.

Mum told her to get off it at once, which she did – give her her due. But it didn't make the assistant any happier; and she gave Angeline a filthy look and then she gave me one for good measure and she turned to give my mum one and all. But she didn't get round to it. My mum can be quite fierce when she wants to be. She's not very good with money, maybe, but she's good at a lot of things. And you don't go giving my mum filthy looks, not just for the sake of it. Because she won't have it, you know. And she won't pretend. She'll just come straight over to you and have it out and say, 'Well then? So what are the filthy looks for?' And if you're not prepared to tell her, it's best not to give her any.

So the shop assistant watered down her filthy looks a bit when it came to my mum; she gave her

16

more of a muddy, vague sort of look.

'Can I help you at all, modom?' she enquired, and she raised one of her eyebrows up, just like it was a little question mark.

Laugh? We almost died when she said that. Because I'd never heard anyone call my mum 'modom' before. I mean, she's hardly a 'modom', is she? I mean, you've seen her, so you'll know.

Anyway, Angeline and me started giggling a bit – till we saw our mum glaring at us, then we stopped. Then, when we were quiet, Mum smiled at the assistant and said, 'We're just pricing some beds, thank you, with a view to buy.'

'Please,' the assistant said, still a bit hoity-toity. 'Be my guest.'

'Is it all right to sit on them to try the mattresses out?' our mum asked.

'Of course,' the assistant replied. 'Feel free to *lie* on them, if you wish. As long as you—'

And you could tell that she was just about to say: 'as long as you take your shoes off first'. But the words never got out. And I knew why. It was because my mum was giving the assistant one of her looks, as if to say, 'Don't you *dare* imply that we are the kind of people who would go lying down on beds in Scottley's without first removing

17

our footwear. If you even so much as *suggest* such a thing . . .'

So the assistant didn't say it. She changed direction in mid-flight and altered what she was about to say to: '– as long as you appreciate that we will be closing in fifteen minutes.'

'Of course,' Mum smiled. 'Don't worry. We shan't be long. It doesn't take us long to make up our minds.'

'Fine,' the assistant said. 'I'll be down at the other end of the department then, conferring with my colleague in Armchairs and Sofas. If you need me, just give me a call.'

'Thank you,' Mum said. 'We will.'

And off the assistant went, to 'confer with her colleague in Armchairs and Sofas' – which I took to mean 'go and have a natter with' – and she left us alone with the beds.

'Whee, Mum,' little Angeline said. 'This is great. Can I go exploring on the beds?'

'Course you can, love,' Mum said. 'Just don't climb up on them with your shoes on or go swinging from the four-posters and hurting yourself.'

So Angeline toddled off to play among the beds, crawling underneath them and then bouncing on the mattresses. But our mum was careful to keep a eye on her and not to let her get too far away. She seemed to be keeping a watchful eye on the assistants down in Armchairs and Sofas too, as if she was waiting for something. Waiting for the time to be right. Waiting – I don't know – almost for a chance to *do* something. Only what?

Mum walked along the aisles between the beds and I followed her, still not entirely happy about a few things. Because you see, it wasn't just the time of day that was bothering me; it wasn't just that we were buying a bed; and it wasn't just that we were buying it from Scottley's, there was something else too.

It was the suitcase.

That's right. The enormous suitcase. It was sort of famous in our family, the suitcase, and whenever it came out from the wardrobe or wherever, you felt that something very important was about to happen.

I suppose that in many ways the suitcase was a bit of a sign, and whenever Mum started packing it, you always knew we were on the move. Well, not always. Sometimes she'd just pack it for the sake of it, and when we asked her why and if it meant we were moving again – because we didn't half get fed up with moving, I don't mind telling you – she'd say, 'No, not necessarily – just dreaming.'

Because she was, our mum, she was always dreaming. And sometimes she'd share her dreams with us and they were pretty good dreams too. We could listen to them for hours, really, as she'd tell us all about this place we were going to have out in the country, with sort of honeysuckle, I think she said it was, in the garden and roses round the door. Or maybe it was honeysuckle round the door and roses in the garden. It was one or the other, I don't really remember which.

I don't know why Mum was so keen on the country though, because she'd never really lived there and I don't think she knew one end of a cow from the other. And even if we *had* ever gone to the country, we'd have been there about five minutes and then she'd have started getting the big suitcase out again. And she'd have said how nice the city was, or how nice Alaska was or how nice the Sahara Desert was, and how she wished she lived there instead.

She's got itchy feet our mum, you see. She says as much herself. And she's got a gypsy in her soul too. Itchy feet and a gypsy in her soul. And the first time she said this to little Angeline, about her having itchy feet, the next thing she knew, Angeline had taken Mum's shoes off and she was scratching away at Mum's feet like nobody's business. And when Mum said, 'Angeline, what are you doing down there?' Angeline just looked up and said, 'I'm trying to get the itchy feet to go away, Mum, so we won't need the big suitcase and have to move any more. And then when the itchy feet have gone, maybe if we buy all the gypsy's clothes-pegs, he'll go away too and we won't have to move house ever again.' But Mum just looked at her, a bit sort of sad; like she was sorry for the way she was, but she couldn't really help herself.

'I'm afraid they don't go away like that, Angeline, love,' she said. 'It's not that kind of scratching that makes itchy feet go away. It's moving on and seeing new places, that's the only cure for itchy feet that I know. And as for that gypsy – well, once he's in your soul, you become a bit of a gypsy yourself. And you can't ever really get rid of him, no more than you could change the colour of your skin.'

So I don't reckon Mum can help it really, to be

honest. And I don't say it's bad either. It's just how she is. And after all, no one says you're bad for staying put, so why should you be bad for moving on? I don't see that one's righter or better than the other, they're just different, that's all.

It is much easier if you do stay put, though. At least I think so. For a start you don't have to be packing and unpacking all the time. And you don't have to keep starting new schools and making new friends all the time – and losing the friends you've just made and probably never seeing them again.

Because we have, really; we've been to loads of schools – or at least I have. And little Angeline, well, she's been to more playgroups and nurseries and what-have-you than most people have had hot dinners – or cold dinners, come to that. And we've had a lot of cold dinners too. Quite a few, in our time. In fact we've probably had more cold dinners than most people have had hot dinners, and that's a fact.

I'll tell you what the hardest part is, about going to all the various schools. It's fitting in and catching up, that's the difficult bit. Because they've always done what you haven't and they know things that you don't, and it's a terrible job trying to keep up and to fit in with new ways of doing things all the time. Because every school's different, you know. They might look pretty similar on the outside, but they're not inside, not really.

CHAPTER THREE

Anyway, it was the big suitcase I was telling you about, wasn't it, and how it always made a regular appearance whenever Mum's feet started getting itchy and whenever that gypsy started moving around in her soul.

It wasn't always the gypsy and the itchy feet though. Sometimes it was money. Mum would never say anything, but you'd just get this feeling that she was having trouble paying all the bills. Because no one works harder than our mum, no one at all, and you wouldn't believe all these arrangements she has to make to get me to school and to get little Angeline looked after while she goes and does a job. And then if one of us is ill she has to take time off work. And so the jobs never really last, you see, not for that long; or they aren't very good ones anyway and they don't pay much money.

So sometimes we have to move even when we'd all prefer to stay. And when that happens we usually move quite late in the day, normally when it's getting dark. It's usually after tea, just when we're thinking we'll have a quiet night in with our comics and books or have a game of something, suddenly Mum'll get out the big suitcase and she'll say, 'You know, I can feel my itchy feet coming on again and I really don't think I can fight them a moment longer. I'm just going to have to scratch them by a good move to somewhere else. Now, who's coming with me?' Well, we were hardly going to say we *weren't* coming with her, were we? We could hardly be left behind on our own, me and little Angeline. Especially not when Mum was going off with the big suitcase with all our things in it.

Mind you, little Angeline had a few fits every now and again. Once she went totally bananas and she stomped all over the place yelling, 'I'm *not*, I'm *not* coming with you. I like it here and I'm fed up moving. And I don't care if you *have* got itchy feet or a gypsy in your socks or wherever he's supposed to be. I'm *not* coming this time. I'm staying *here*. So there!' But although I might have felt a bit the same, I didn't dare say so. And so once Angeline's tantrum was over, we gathered up our best and most valuable possessions and packed them away in the big suitcase. Then we put our warm coats on and walked off into the night; off along the pavements, often glistening with rain. And all the traffic was roaring by us, all the buses and cars and taxi-cabs. And there we were, me and Mum and little Angeline and the big suitcase, all going off down the road together to who-knew-where.

Now, the big suitcase had wheels on it and a handle for pulling it along. So you didn't actually have to carry it all the time, which was just as well or it would have yanked your arm off. It's a really good suitcase too, and I don't know where Mum got it from, but it's very smart looking. It cheers you up sometimes, just to see it. Because it looks so solid and important and just like a proper suitcase, like people would have for a real journey – like going on an aeroplane or something. And you know things can't be that bad, not when you've got a suitcase like that.

To be honest, I don't know that Mum really knew where we were going half the time. There we'd be, traipsing down the street with the big suitcase, and it seemed as if Mum was just looking for somewhere for us to go, for a sign in a window saying *Rooms To Let*. And often we'd walk around for hours – or it seemed like hours – and little Angeline would almost be falling asleep on her feet, and I'd maybe have to give her a piggy back for as long as I could – which wasn't that long, as I'd be tired too.

Sometimes we'd stop and all sit down on the big suitcase for a rest. Once, while we were doing that, I remember that this police car stopped and these two policemen came out and walked over – even though we hadn't done anything wrong. Because there's no law against sitting on a suitcase, is there? Not as far as I know. Not that I'm in the police, of course; but I can't hardly imagine that would be wrong, not sitting on a suitcase.

But they seemed quite nice, really, the two policemen, and they asked Mum if they could help her, and then the three of them went a few steps away for a *word in private*. Grown-ups are always saying that when they don't want you listening. A *word in private* they call it. And they usually want it *in private* because it's *you* they're talking about.

I couldn't hear much of what they were saying, but I did hear one of the policemen say 'social services' and my mum got angry then and said something like, 'I'm never going *there* again to be insulted. No thank you!' Then one of the policemen said, 'We can't possibly leave you with two children like this.' And Mum said something about 'putting up with her sister for a while'. Well, it was the first I'd heard about her having any sisters. But the policemen seemed satisfied, so they drove away and left us alone with our suitcase.

'Whereabouts does your sister live, Mum?' I asked, when the policemen had gone.

But 'never you mind,' was all she would say. And so on we went, on through the streets, looking at the windows for *Rooms To Let* signs; until eventually we found somewhere, and in we'd go, and there we'd stay – until Mum got itchy feet again or until the gypsy in her soul got restless.

Now Mum had a special expression for when we'd suddenly move house at night. Moonlight flits, she called them. She could make them sound really great and exciting too, just like it was a proper adventure with jungles and crocodiles, or something like that.

'Come on,' she'd say. 'Tell you what, let's pack the big suitcase and all do a moonlight flit. What do you say, Livvy? What do you think, Angeline?'

The first time she suggested it, of course we

28

both went bananas and said, 'Yeah! Great! Let's do a moonlight flit. Let's all go moonlight flitting! It'll be fantastic!' Though we had no idea what a moonlight flit was at all.

As time went by though, and once we'd done two or three moonlight flits, we got a bit fed up with them. And instead of getting all excited about them like we had done the first time, we began to pull long faces and say, 'Oh, must we?' and 'Do we have to, Mum? Do we have to go moonlight flitting? Can't we just do a bit of moonlight staying-put instead?'

But it was usually too late. The big suitcase would already be packed and we'd have no choice than to go moonlight flitting, whether we wanted to or not.

Don't get the wrong impression, mind. I mean, we never went hungry or anything like that. Mum always took care of us. She was the best mum ever. And you couldn't say you weren't wanted, because Mum would always be telling you that she loved you, twenty or thirty times a day.

We've lived in some funny places though. We must have lived all over. In fact we even lived in a bus once. Not the Number 23, in case you're wondering, but an old bus that didn't work properly. And then we lived in an ambulance – not a fast one, mind, more one that didn't go anywhere. Then for a while we lived in an old railway carriage, and after that we lived in a wigwam, over in the woods on the other side of the river. A tepee, my mum called it. We weren't on our own though, we were with lots of other people and my mum said they were called travellers. But I don't know why, because they never seemed to travel anywhere. Most of the time they just stayed put. Stay-putters, they should have been called. When the winter came, it got so cold in the wigwam that my mum started to pack the big suitcase again. She said it was no place for little Angeline, not with her bad chest, and that she needed a proper four walls round her to keep her warm. So we left the wigwam and went off to live in a room back in town. I suppose that was the first of many rooms, and we've been going from room to room and from place to place ever since.

And now we're here.

Anyway, the reason I'm saying all this isn't just for the sake of rambling on. Because I can see you're yawning a bit . . . oh, tired, are you? Yes, it has been a long day. No, the reason I'm saying this about the suitcase is just to let you know that when we walked into Scottley's Bedding Department that afternoon, with our big suitcase in tow, I already had my suspicions that something might be up.

Now Mum hadn't said anything that afternoon about her feet getting itchy again or about the gypsy wanting to go wandering, but she went and packed the suitcase just the same. When we asked why, and whether it had anything to do with the men who'd come to the door that morning, she said, 'Oh no, not at all'. No, she said the reason we had to take the suitcase with us was that there had been a lot of burglaries in the area recently and it wasn't safe to leave your valuables at home. She said the police were advising everyone to take all their valuables with them whenever they went out – especially if they had a big suitcase. Which, luckily, we did.

When you thought about it though, it was a bit hard to believe. Because, I mean, what if you had a big telly? Or a valuable piece of antique furniture? Or a nice stereo system? Or a computer even? You'd never get that lot into a suitcase, would you? And I couldn't really believe that the police were telling everyone to carry their tellies about in suitcases rather than leave them at home, in case burglars broke in and stole them. I mean, that seemed like taking security just a bit too far, to my mind.

But Mum was in charge, so we did what she said. It's best not to argue with her sometimes, especially when she has that 'don't argue with me' look. So if she said the police were telling everyone to carry their tellies round in suitcases, then that's how it was, and no question.

When we went into Scottley's with our big suitcase in tow, I must admit that the doorman, Mr Whiskers, did give us a bit of a sniffy look. We didn't expect him to be at the side door because he was usually at the front. But there he was, with his great big whiskers sticking out from under his nose, and he took one look at our suitcase and said, 'Perhaps you would prefer to leave that in the left luggage office while you shop in Scottley's.'

'Yes, perhaps I would,' Mum agreed. 'But on the other hand, perhaps I wouldn't.'

And before he could waggle his whiskers at her again, she was off with the suitcase and with us in tow heading for the escalator, and we were on our way up to the Bedding Department.

Now, as soon as we entered the Bedding Department, I noticed that Mum did what I thought was a rather funny thing.

. . . She hid the suitcase. No, she did. Yes, that's right. Just as we came into the department, she sort of rolled the suitcase behind a wardrobe that was on display there. She rolled it out of sight and when she saw me watching her, she said, 'Be safer there and more out of the way until we've decided on which bed we want. No need to mention it to anyone.'

But to be honest, I don't think she left it there to be out of the way. I think she put it there because she didn't want the Bedding Department assistant to see it. Just in case it gave her ideas. Just as if . . . well, you know . . . as if she might have thought we'd come to stay or something.

So anyway, there we were. Saturday evening, a quarter to six, in the Bedding Department at Scottley's department store, our big suitcase hidden behind a wardrobe and us shopping for a new bed. A new expensive bed. Us, who could hardly afford a drink and a scone in Scottley's café, let alone an ice cream sundae in their ice cream parlour. (And wait until I tell you about

Scottley's ice cream parlour, now that *is* something!)

It just didn't make sense to me, no sense at all, and I began to grow more and more anxious as the hands on the wall-clock moved nearer and nearer to six.

At ten to, there was an announcement over the intercom.

'Scottley's department store will be closing in ten minutes. We repeat, the doors will be closing in ten minutes. Will customers wishing to make purchases please make their way to the nearest till. Would other customers kindly make their way down towards the nearest exit. Scottley's will be open again at nine a.m. on Monday morning. Thank you for your custom. And have a happy weekend.'

But Mum made no sign of heading for any exits or going towards any tills. She just went on through the Bedding Department, prodding a mattress here, testing a pillow there, just like she was really serious about buying a brand new bed. She seem totally absorbed in it too. But I also had a feeling that she was watching the assistants and was just waiting for the moment when their backs would be turned and we would be out of sight.

And while she did this, little Angeline hopped about as happy as ever, just like the Bedding Department was one great playroom, and there was all the time in the world and not a care in it.

'Mum,' I hissed at her. 'Mum! It's ten to. They just made an announcement. We ought to be leaving now. The man said.'

'Never mind what the man said, Livvy, I just want to take a look at this bed.'

'But Mum . . .' I went on, and I began to get really flustered and agitated. Because I do like to do things properly and to stick by the rules. Maybe it's because I'm the eldest, I don't know. But I hate it when things are all shapeless and wishy-washy, and I do like to know where I stand. So when they say you have to leave by six o'clock, I like to leave by six o'clock – or even a little bit earlier if possible – and that's the kind of person I am. I like to be correct. It's maybe a good thing in some ways and maybe a fault in others. I wish I could be more relaxed sometimes and take things more easily, the way little Angeline does. Maybe if she'd been born first and I'd been born second, I would be like that. But I wasn't. So I'm me and she's her and Mum's Mum and you're you and we're all ourselves, and that's the way it is.

The clock hands moved to five to six. The 'time to go' announcement was repeated over the intercom. Yet still Mum made no signs of leaving or that she was even aware of the deadline.

'Mum,' I all but pleaded, tugging at her coat, 'Mum, we ought to go now before we get into trouble. We really ought to. Or the man with the whiskers will be round. Mum!'

But instead of getting annoyed with me, as she sometimes did when I got anxious, she just smiled and said, 'It's okay, Livvy, loads of time yet, no hurry.' Then she looked up to where the two shop assistants had been talking to each other at the far end of the department, but they had both gone. I didn't know where and I was sure they'd be back any second to check that the place was empty.

The instant Mum saw that they were gone, she called little Angeline over and said, 'Angeline, Livvy, how about we all play a little game?'

Game? I thought. What was she doing wanting to play *games*? It was three minutes to six in Scottley's Bedding Department on a Saturday night. We had to leave the store in three minutes' time – with or without our bed – and here was my mum wanting to play *games*.

But little Angeline thought it was a great idea.

'Okay, Mum,' she said. 'What shall we play?'

'Let's have a game,' Mum said, 'of Hide Under the Bed.'

'Whoopee!' little Angeline cried, dead keen immediately. 'How do you play it?'

'Yes, Mum,' I said, giving her a very cold and sort of knowing look. 'How *do* you play Hide Under the Bed . . . as if I couldn't guess,' I added, under my breath.

'Well, Angeline,' Mum said, 'it couldn't be easier. You and me and Livvy are going to hide under the beds here. And the two ladies who were over there a moment ago are going to come and maybe have a look for us. But we're going to see if we can keep very, very still –'

'Just like Sleeping Lions,' Angeline said.

'Yes,' Mum said, 'just like Sleeping Lions. And we're going to stay ever so still and not make a sound, not even when they turn the lights off. And then when they do, we're not going to be afraid of the dark. Because it shouldn't be *that* dark, as they're bound to leave a few lights on. Then when the ladies are gone, we're going to tiptoe out from under the beds, still keeping really quiet, and then we all get a sweetie.' And Mum took a bag of chocolate buttons from her pocket, just to show that she really had some.

'Goody, sweeties,' little Angeline said.

'Yes,' Mum agreed. 'And the person who I think has been quietest of all gets *double* sweeties.'

'That'll be me!' Angeline said. 'That'll be me, me, *me*!'

'Shhhh!' Mum said, looking anxiously over her shoulder as if afraid that one of the assistants might hear. 'You've got to be very quiet from now on, or you won't get double sweeties.'

'I'll be quiet then,' Angeline promised. 'Very quiet.'

'Okay. So let's get under this big bed here now,' Mum said, 'and we'll be as quiet as mice. And when everyone's gone and the lights are out, we'll all have some sweeties. And there will be double sweeties for the winner of Hide Under the Bed.'

'Great,' Angeline said. 'Come on then, let's hide.' She wriggled away under the bed so as to be the first one there, so as to be the best at Hide Under the Bed and to get double sweeties.

But I'm too old to be taken in like that. I'm not saying I can't be taken in at all, but I can't be taken in that way. I knew as soon as Mum mentioned the game of Hide Under the Bed just what she was up to. I knew immediately why she'd packed the big suitcase. I knew why we'd come to Scottley's at almost six o'clock on a Saturday night, just when they were about to close. Oh yes, I knew what we were doing there. I knew why we were hiding under the bed all right.

'Mum,' I hissed at her, 'you don't mean it. Tell me you don't. You don't mean it, do you? You can't be serious?'

'Under the bed, Livvy,' she told me, 'come on, or I'll get angry.'

So under the bed I had to go. And there I was. Me and Mum under the big four-poster bed, with little Angeline between us trying not to sneeze or snort or laugh or giggle, so as to be the one who got double sweeties.

Oh, I knew what we were doing there all right. We hadn't come to play Hide Under the Bed. We were there for another reason entirely. We were moving in.

We had come to live at Scottley's.

CHAPTER FOUR

Well, I don't mind telling you, I was scared absolutely rigid. And as the three of us lay there under the big four-poster bed – with little Angeline acting like it was the biggest lark going since she'd been on the merry-go-round – all I could think to myself was: *Mum, you've really gone and done it this time, you really have. You really have gone and done it.* Because she's had some schemes in her time, my mum has, but never anything like this. This was the scheme to end all schemes, this was.

So anyway, we lay there for what felt like ages, just like statues under the bed. The department seemed to empty quite quickly. At first we heard voices and footsteps and people calling to each other, saying 'Good night' and 'Have a nice weekend' or 'See you later,' just like they'd arranged to meet up somewhere and go for a dance or to see a film.

I thought that was funny actually, the shop assistants meeting up like that. You'd think they'd have seen enough of each other for six days of the week without going out together of an evening as well. It also seemed funny to be saying 'Have a nice weekend,' because there wasn't much of it left, really, was there? Not if it was already Saturday night. There was only Sunday and then it would be back to work. Didn't seem like much of a weekend to me. More like half a weekend at the most.

Anyway, first there were the voices and then footsteps, and then there was darkness. Or rather, more darkness. It was already pretty dark under the bed, but you could still see the glow of the lights in the shop. But then someone must have turned them off, and I had the feeling that the assistants had really gone and we were all alone in the Bedding Department.

'Mum—' I began.

'Shhh!' she whispered, loud enough to wake the dead. 'Not yet!' And she actually clamped her hand right over my mouth. I almost bit her, I was so annoyed. But I didn't. I didn't think it would be a very good idea.

We waited under the bed a while longer. Soon

the whole store had gone quiet. It was odd really, a great big place like that; you'd imagine it would have taken hours and hours for a shop that big to calm down. But no, it went really quiet in no more than ten or fifteen minutes.

But when your eyes got used to the change in light, you realised that the shop wasn't *that* dark at all. Down on the ground floor it was almost as clear as day in places, because they had all the window displays down there – the ones for which Scottley's was so rightfully famous – and they glowed as bright as neon and stayed on all night long. The electricity bills must have been enormous, that was all I could think. It just seemed like sheer extravagance to me, because my mum was always on at us to turn the lights off and save money.

Anyway, after about ten minutes or quarter of an hour or so, little Angeline began to squirm about and to get really restless and uncomfortable, and not even the prospect of double sweeties could have kept her still much longer. So finally, when she thought the coast was clear, my mum said, 'Okay, Hide Under the Bed is over. We can all get out now and decide who the winner is.'

So out we got and of course the winner was

little Angeline, as we'd all known it would be – apart from little Angeline maybe, who didn't know it was a foregone conclusion – and we sat on the bed and shared out the packet of chocolate buttons and Angeline had double. I can remember sucking away at my share of the chocolates and thinking to myself that if a few chocolate buttons was all we were getting for tea, it was going to be a pretty long and hungry night.

As we sat there eating, me wondering what was going to happen next, Mum got very particular about the mattress we were perched on and she said that on no account were we to get any chocolate on to it as it wasn't our mattress and we ought to respect other people's things, and she brushed invisible crumbs off it.

So we all sat and ate our chocolate buttons really daintily, with our hands under our chins to catch the bits, as if we had guests round. (Not that *that* happened often. We never had guests round. And it was even less likely now.)

'What'll we do now, Mum?' little Angeline said when she'd finished her chocolate buttons. 'Now what game shall we play?'

'Well, let me think,' Mum said, and she rested her chin on her hand, just like she really was thinking. But it looked more like acting thinking than real thinking to me. And then she acted having a brain-wave and said, 'I know, Angel! I know what we can do! It looks to me as if everyone's gone and we've been left all on our own. So why don't we have a game of Live In the Shop for a while? What do you say?'

'Yeah!' yelled little Angeline. 'Yeah, yeah, yeah! Live In the Shop yeah! How do we do that, Mum?'

'Well,' Mum said, 'what we do, Angel, is to make up some of the beds here for us to sleep in, and we can stay here in the nice big warm shop all tonight and all tomorrow and all tomorrow night, and then when it's Monday morning, we can say, "Thank you Mr Shop—"'

'Thank you, Mr Shop,' little Angeline echoed.

'Thank you very much, Mr Shop, for letting us stay with you.'

'Thank you, Mr Shop,' little Angeline said again, and she went on saying it until I felt like stuffing a sock in her mouth. 'Thank you, Mr Shop. Thank you, Mrs Bedding Department.'

'That's right, Angel,' Mum said. 'We say, "Thank you Mr Shop," and then we take the big suitcase and we all go off to the council offices, to the Housing Department, and we see if they haven't got a nice flat for us to live in yet, like they promised – instead of another of those horrible rooms in those awful hotels, like when we had to share with the other lady. Remember?'

I remembered it all right. How could I forget? It wasn't that the other lady wasn't nice; she was and so were her three children. It just meant that there were seven of us, all sleeping in this one room. I didn't like that at all. On balance, I'd rather be in Scottley's.

I wasn't just prepared to leave it at that though. And when I saw that Mum was *seriously* intending us all to spend the night in Scottley's Bedding Department I began to get very anxious indeed. Super anxious.

True, one part of me was relieved that she was only planning on us being there until Monday morning. But most of me felt that we shouldn't be there at all and that this time Mum had gone too far, and that she was really going to land us in the most terrible trouble and the hottest of hot water. Which I suppose she has done in a way.

Anyway, I didn't want to worry little Angeline – not any more than Mum did; so I just said casually, 'Mum, might I have a word with you *in private* for a moment?' But of course little Angeline wanted a word *in private* too then. So in order to keep her occupied, I had a sudden brain-wave myself, and I said, 'Angeline, how would you like to come up to Scottley's Toy Department with me for a moment and see if we can't get you a toy to play with? It won't be to keep, mind, just a loan. But would you like that?'

'Oh yes,' she said. 'Great. Come on.'

'I'll be back in a minute, Mum,' I said. 'And then I'd like to speak to you please, *in private*, about one or two things. All right?'

'Okay, Livvy,' she said, quite cheerfully, just as if getting locked in Scottley's on a Saturday evening and sleeping overnight in the Bedding Department were things that happened all the time. 'Okay, Livvy, you take Angeline up to the Toy Department. Don't try to use the lifts, mind.'

'I wasn't going to,' I snapped, and I almost added, 'I'm not stupid and irresponsible, you know,' and then I almost added again, 'not like some I could mention.' But I didn't. I just kept my thoughts to myself.

'Oh, and don't take any toys out of any boxes,' Mum called after us, as I took Angeline's hand and began to lead her away. 'Just use the toys that are already out on display, the ones they use for demonstrations. Don't touch anything brand new or go spoiling anything.'

'I *know*, Mum!' I said. 'I wasn't going to open any boxes!' She does get me exasperated at times.

'See you in a little while then,' Mum said. 'Take your time. No hurry. It'll give me a chance to make the beds up.'

I stopped in my tracks.

'Make the beds up, Mum? What do you mean make the beds up?'

'Oh, I won't use anything new,' she said. 'I'm not going to open up any new packets of sheets or use any new blankets. We'll just borrow what's on display, that's all. You can choose your beds if you like. I think I'll have the big four-poster, myself. What do you two fancy? How about the bunk beds?'

Just the mention of bunk beds got little Angeline so excited I thought that she might explode.

'Bunk beds!' she went, jumping up and down. 'Bunk beds, bunk beds, bunky-wunky-funky beds! And baggsy me on the top.'

Well, normally I'd have given her a bit of an argument about who was going to go on the top, because I like the top bunk as well. The view's always better from the top bunk and the air's usually a bit fresher too. Whenever we'd slept in bunk beds before we'd always tossed a coin first; heads or tails for who was going to go on top. But this time I just didn't care. She could have the top bunk. All I wanted right then was to get out of Scottley's and never set eyes on the place again.

'Bunk bed, bunk bed,' little Angeline kept going. 'Chunky-lunky-hunky bed! Me on the top.'

'All right,' I growled at her. 'Be quiet. You can have the top. Okay? Satisfied?'

But I must admit though that those bunk beds they had on display in Scottley's, they were lovely. They weren't just your ordinary, rickety old bunk beds like you usually get. They were built like a small ship, with a top cabin and a lower cabin, and they had beautiful stencils on the sides of portholes and of sails. And they had these quilts on them too, which Mum said we could have as long as we were careful and didn't have 'any little accidents' as she called them, and she gave little Angeline a meaningful look then. She didn't single her out by name, but she knew and I knew that *I* wasn't going to have any 'little accidents', not at my age. If anyone was going to, it was Angeline.

Angeline promised that she wouldn't have any little accidents, nor any big ones neither, not just as long as she could have the top cabin of that beautiful ship-shaped bunk bed with the marvellous pictures on the side and with the warm quilts on it with the big, dreamy clouds on them. Just looking at those clouds made you feel all sleepy. Sleepy and warm and safe.

'Okay,' Mum said. 'You two toddle off to the Toy Department and see if you can't borrow – and I do mean *borrow* – a toy for tonight, and I'll make the beds up. By the time you come back, I should have done all that, and then we can see about finding some supper. Now, where did I leave the big suitcase?'

I suddenly had that feeling of doom again. That feeling of everything being just about to go wrong.

'Mum,' I said. 'Mum, what do you mean about *finding some supper*? Would you mind explaining to me for just one moment exactly how we are going to find—'

'Why don't you take little Angeline to the Toy Department, Livvy?' she said, 'and then we can have our little private talk after. Okay?'

'Okay, Mum,' I said, through gritted teeth. 'But I *do* want a little talk, Mum. I really do. In fact, I might want quite a long talk, about several things. Okay, Mum?'

'Okay, Livvy,' she said, as calm and easy-going as ever, just as though everything was all perfectly normal and there was nothing to worry about at all. 'Okay, we'll have our talk in a while.'

So I took little Angeline's hand and off we went together towards the escalator. I looked back once to see how Mum was getting on. I saw her there, unpacking our night things from the big suitcase, and you know, she was even humming a little tune. She really was. Just like she didn't have a care in the world. And right then, she didn't feel like my mum at all. It felt more as if I was hers.

The escalator wasn't moving. They'd turned it off, of course, when they'd closed the store. The Bedding Department was on the third floor and the Toy Department was up on the fourth. We could have taken the real stairs instead of the unmoving escalator, but I didn't want to. For one thing it would have been the longer way round; for another I thought we might get caught. I was worried that there might still be someone else in the building. Or if not, that the place would be alarmed and that we would set the alarm off if we went out into the stairwell.

As it turned out, the shop *was* alarmed – *and* it

was patrolled. But the alarms and patrols were more there to stop people getting *in*. Not to stop people already inside from wandering around. And if you were careful, you were all right.

Angeline and I walked up the escalator. It felt funny to be on it when it wasn't moving. The steps seemed far apart and rather wide, and I had to help little Angeline up them. I said for a joke, 'We ought to be roped together, Angeline, just like we were climbing a mountain.' And she laughed. Which made me feel happy for a minute. Just because I was worried sick at this new mess Mum had got us into, it didn't mean little Angeline had to worry too.

But as soon as we got to the top of the escalator and entered the dimly lit Toy Department, my worries all disappeared. I forgot all about Mum and the big suitcase and us never having anywhere proper to live, and about Dad being away on the oil wells for so long and him always forgetting our birthdays and Christmas and never remembering to send Mum any money. I forgot all that, because we had something really special. Just us. Just me and little Angeline, just her and me. We had the whole of Scottley's Toy Department all to ourselves.

Can you imagine it? It just went on forever. There were toys as far as you could see. Toys in front, toys behind, toys all round you. Toys and toys and toys! I mean, if you've ever been to Scottley's you'll know what it's like. Even when you go there during the day it seems huge, even when it's full of other people. But at night, when it's only half-lit with the red glow of the exit signs and the fire alarms and with the light still on from some of the displays, and when you've got the whole place to yourself, it really is just magic.

You might think it would be creepy with all those boxes of dolls and all those heaps of cuddly toys staring at you. But it's not creepy at all. It's just wonderful. It's like the biggest Santa's grotto in the whole world. Almost like it was the *real* Santa's grotto, where all the Christmas toys were kept in preparation for December the twenty-fifth.

Oh, but they had everything there, I really do mean *everything*. They even had little cars for children – *real* cars that you could drive on *real* roads (well, roads where there was no traffic) and they cost thousands of pounds. No exaggeration. I saw the price tickets on them. *Two thousand pounds* one of them cost. Can you imagine that? Two thousand pounds just for a *toy*!

Well, some very rich people must shop in Scottley's, that's all I can say. Imagine having a mum and dad who could buy you a two-thousand-pound toy! My mum would have had trouble buying us a two-pound toy. Not that I'd ever have swapped her – not for the most expensive toy or for any other mum; but it did make you wonder how some other people lived.

Anyway, me and little Angeline went and sat in the cars – they were on display and we didn't do any damage – and we went 'Beep, beep,' and pretended to go fast. Then we got fed up with that and Angeline wanted to look at the dolls and to choose one to take back to the Bedding Department with her. So off we went to find one.

Well, I tell you, that Toy Department was so big that you could have lost yourself in it and never have been found again, not for days. So I gave little Angeline strict instructions that we weren't to be separated. But I was still afraid I might lose her. So when I saw this toy walkie-talkie set on display, I gave her one half and I took the other. So that way we could stay in touch, even when we couldn't see each other. We went off on our own separate ways for a while then, saying things into the walkie-talkie like, 'I am now just passing along by the bicycles. Where are you?' Or 'I am moving along now by the jigsaws and expect to be down by the Lego man in about thirty seconds, over.'

It was great. And then we found some torches – also on display, because we had strict rules that we wouldn't touch *anything* unless it was out on display. No taking things out of boxes or damaging anything, and that was a definite.

Well, we found these torches called Space Laser Beams which gave out light in all different colours. And we went all over the Toy Department, sliding down the slides and hiding in the Wendy Houses and all sorts, flashing our Space Laser Beams at each other and growling down our walkie-talkies, saying, 'Captain Kirk to the Starship Enterprise' and 'Beam me up Scotty' (which is what they say on the old-fashioned *Star Trek* programme on TV, the original one that is, in case you don't know).

After a while though, I thought that maybe we ought to stop messing about with the torches. Because what if somebody out in the street looked up and saw these lights flashing about inside Scottley's? I got a bit worried then and asked Angeline to give me her torch and we returned them to where we'd found them, and the walkie-talkies too, and then we went to find her a doll.

Well, there were dolls galore. Some of them were almost as big as Angeline, some were even bigger. And the things they could *do*! They could cry, snore, snort, gurgle, walk, talk, open and close their eyes, burp, sing, whistle, make rude noises, and some of them could even do wees – though you had to fill them up with water first. There were so many out on display that you were totally spoilt for choice. Angeline kept picking them up, one after the other, saying,' 'I'll have this one,' then she'd spot a better one and say, 'No, I won't, I'll have this one instead, this is cuddlier.' And then she'd choose yet another one, because it had nicer hair or it could make more noises, or one thing or another.

Anyway, while she tried all the dolls and was making her mind up about which one to borrow, I decided to have a look at the children's computers. I switched one on and I got it going, and I was trying out this really good painting game and I was really getting involved in it, when suddenly I noticed this shadow coming up behind me. And before I could turn or even open my mouth to scream, a hand fell on to my shoulder and a voice said, 'I thought you wanted to have a serious talk, Livvy. Well, you seem to have got distracted.'

It was Mum. We'd forgotten all about her. We'd been having such a good time with all the toys that the serious talk I wanted to have with her as a matter of some urgency had gone right out of my mind.

She stood there grinning at me. I felt a bit annoyed with myself, to be honest, for getting so involved with the toys; and with Mum too, for gloating over it, as if to say, 'And I thought you were the *sensible* one – ha, ha!'

I turned the computer off and called to Angeline.

'Mum's here,' I said.

'I've made your beds up,' Mum told us. 'Have you chosen a toy, Angel? But remember it's only on a loan. It's not to keep.'

'I want this one,' Angeline said. And she held up an all-talking, all-walking, all-singing, all-dancing, wee-weeing doll, that cost a small fortune to buy. 'I want her to keep me company tonight.'

'You'll have to make up another bed for that one,' I told her.

'It's all right,' Angeline said, 'I'll budge up and make room. I'll call her Christabel.'

'Okay,' Mum said. 'Come on then, let's go down.'

So Angeline picked up the enormous doll and

we all went back down the escalator. The doll was too big for her to carry on her own, so she took its head and I took its feet and we managed it between us.

We got back down to Beds and Bedding and saw that Mum had made up the bunk beds for us and the four-poster for herself – it all looked very cosy too. And it was nice and warm. I think they must have left the heating on all night in Scottley's, or maybe it just stayed warm with all the stuff in there. It was certainly warmer than our last place, with the tiny electric fire for us to huddle round. I know that.

Angeline put her doll up in the top bunk (with a little help from me) and I said, 'Why don't you snuggle up a minute with her, Angeline, while I have a talk with Mum?' But she wouldn't. Instead she said what I'd been dreading she'd say, although I was feeling the same way myself.

'Mum,' she said, 'can't we have some supper? I am very, very hungry.'

Now, I knew Mum didn't have any food and I knew we couldn't exactly nip out to the fish and chip shop – even if we had the money for fish and chips, which seemed extremely unlikely. In a way we were locked up inside Scottley's and I was sure there was no way we could get out without setting the alarms off. The only way out as far as I could tell was through one of the emergency exits, and I knew for a fact that they were wired up to the alarms, as I'd seen and heard it happen once when a lady in the shop tried to get out through an emergency door by mistake.

So if we couldn't get out for chips, and if the chips couldn't get in, then either we were going to go hungry or –

'Are you hungry, Angeline?' Mum said. 'So am I a bit. I know, let's go and see what we can find. Come on.'

'Mum,' I said, 'I really would like to have a *very* serious talk with you, I really would.'

'Later, Livvy,' she smiled, 'when we've had something to eat. Let's all go together and see what there is, shall we?'

And before I could object any further, she was off hand-in-hand with little Angeline, and it was either stay there on my own and get nothing to eat or go with them and see what we might find. So I went with them. I didn't see what else I could do.

We walked down the escalator to the second floor.

There were ladies everywhere in beautiful clothes – well, plastic ladies – and there were racks of blouses and skirts and gorgeous dresses and everything you could imagine. Then down we went to the first floor. This was full of plastic men in elegant suits and expensive jackets, and there were loads of silks ties in all the colours you could dream off. And then we went down the next escalator and then we were on the ground floor.

The first thing I noticed was the smell of scent. The escalator stairs had taken us down into the Perfumery section, and the smell of all those different perfumes was absolutely out of this world. It could have smelt terrible, all those different fragrances, all mingled together. But it wasn't, it was marvellous. It was so sweet it made you feel quite light-headed.

'This is great, Mum,' little Angeline said, as we walked through the department. 'This was a great idea of yours to come and live here—'

'Live?' I said. '*Live*! We haven't come to live here, Angeline, not by—'

But Mum shushed me up and she leant over and whispered in my ear, 'Not in front of little Angeline, Livvy. You and I'll have our talk later. Okay?'

So I just had to smile and go along with it, same as I always do. Just like I seem to spend half my life doing.

'Mum,' said Angeline, who had stopped at one of the counters and was reaching up for a bottle. 'What's a tester?'

'It's a sample of perfume,' Mum said, just grabbing the bottle in time before Angeline dropped it and smashed it all over the marble-tiled floor. 'It's for customers to try out to see if they like it enough to buy a whole bottle.'

'Can I try it?' she said.

'I don't see why not,' Mum nodded. 'It does say *Tester – Free Sample*. Why not? Just mind it doesn't go in your eyes.'

So Angeline had a squirt of perfume on her wrist. And then she had squirts of several other perfumes as well. Then Mum went looking for one particular perfume and when she found the tester for it, she had a squirt of that. And she took a really deep breath of it, just like it was anaesthetic or laughing gas, and she went all ladylike and waved her arms about like a ballet dancer and said, 'I feel like a million dollars. I've always loved that perfume, but I've never been able to afford it.'

Well, I don't know how she could have loved it

if she'd never had it, but I didn't bother to ask. To be honest, I was having a few squirts with the testers myself, trying to find a perfume I liked. But there were so many of them, it was hard to remember which was which.

We must have spent a good twenty minutes there with all the testers, and by the time we had finished, I don't know what we smelt like. We had perfume here and perfume there and perfume all over. We had so much expensive perfume on us it was hard not to swank. And I think we all felt like a million dollars, not just Mum – so that made three million dollars between us, when you added us up, which is quite a lot of money.

But we only used the testers, that was all. And we really only had a tiny drop, because a little smell does go a long way – as I'd noticed for myself, back when Angeline was a baby, because she only had little nappies then but they didn't half pong. And if you've ever let a tiny stink bomb off in shop – not that I ever have, of course – you'll know that you can smell it for miles. So smells are a bit like balloons, really. They start off small, but they can get very big.

Honestly though, we never opened any boxes or bottles that weren't open already. And that's the truth. We didn't steal anything, we really didn't. Not all the time we were there in Scottley's. I don't think we took a single thing that wasn't there for everyone. Not one single thing. Except maybe for things that would have been thrown away anyway. And if we ever did take anything that wouldn't have been thrown away anyway, well, I think we've paid for it. I really think we have. Two or three times over.

CHAPTER FIVE

Right. So there we were, all smelling like models and having a great time in the Perfumery Department. Quite honestly, we'd totally forgotten about being hungry, but then it suddenly came back to us, like a big empty space where your stomach ought to be.

'I'm starving, Mum,' Angeline said. So was I, and so was Mum maybe because she said, 'Come on then. Follow me. And keep well away from the windows. We don't want to be seen from the street.' And off we went towards the Food Hall.

Now, if you know what Scottley's is like, you'll realise that it's quite easy to stay away from the windows because it's like rooms within rooms there, and lots of the departments don't have any windows at all.

So we weren't that worried about being spotted by anyone outside who might be peering in doing some window-shopping, and we made our way confidently through the Perfumery Department, past the Handbags section, across into the Biscuits Department and then on past the chocolate counters.

Oh, but the Chocolate Department, it's just amazing. And to be there all on your own, just us, surrounded by all this chocolate, piled half the way up to the ceiling! And all the chocolate displays and chocolate counters seem to go on for miles. They had every kind of chocolate imaginable there, from all over the world, probably from outer space too. Yes, I think they must have chocolate there from the far reaches of the universe. There were little delicate chocolates with fancy tops; there were big, huge slabs that could have fed an army; there were chocolates in boxes, loose chocolates, dark chocolates, milk chocolates, chocolates with soft centres, chocolates with toffee inside, chocolates made entirely out of chocolate with chocolate all the way through and extra chocolate on top – there were all the chocolates you could ever imagine times ten.

And the smell. The smell of all that chocolate was so strong and sweet and overpowering that we could barely smell the perfume we had on any more. It was as if the chocolate was a perfume, a perfume in its own right. And little Angeline and I just stopped right there, in the middle of the Chocolate Department, just like we'd died and gone to chocolate heaven and were surrounded by chocolate angels.

We breathed in the smell of all that delicious chocolate and it would have been a difficult thing to choose which was the best right then – the Toy Department or the chocolate one. Because you can't eat toys, but you can't really play with chocolate. But we were so hungry that I reckon we'd have come down on the side of the chocolate.

So we stood there, inhaling the chocolate vapours, and we looked at Mum and Mum looked at us, and little Angeline said, 'Oh, Mum, smell all that chocolate . . . oh, Mum, there's so much of it . . . can we? Just a *little* one?'

And it was true, there were so many chocolates on display there – thousands and thousands and thousands of them, possibly even millions – that they'd *never* have missed one, or even two, or even a few hundred.

So little Angeline just stood there making her eyes go all big, like she can do when she really wants something and she's trying to get her own way. And she said, 'Mum – oh, can we? Can we, Mum? *Pleeeeese*?' And when little Angeline goes all big-eyed and says '*Pleeeeese*?' it's almost impossible to refuse her anything.

You could tell that Mum really would have liked to have said, 'Yes, go on, help yourselves, there's plenty there,' because we don't get that many treats, not often. And those chocolate buttons we'd had up in the Bedding Department must have been the first we'd had in weeks. It would have been so easy for Mum to have said yes. But she didn't.

She made a very solemn face instead and said, 'Now listen you two, we mustn't take what isn't ours. Free samples and testers are one thing and using up things that are going to be thrown away anyway is all right too. But taking things that are there to be sold and which we can't pay for – well no, that's not allowed.'

So Angeline started to cry then, to try and make Mum change her mind. But she wouldn't. They can be as stubborn as each other sometimes, Mum and Angeline. And I can be as stubborn as both of them put together. (Not that I am often. Most of the time I just go along with things.) 'No,' she said, 'I'm sorry, Angeline, no chocolates unless we can pay for them, and we can't right now. So come on, let's go on to the Food Hall and see if we can't find something proper to eat.'

So off we went, leaving the piles of wonderful chocolates behind us, little Angeline crying her head off because she couldn't have any and Mum trying to shush her until finally she stopped and said, 'Look, Angeline, if you don't stop crying, somebody outside will hear us. And they'll tell somebody else and then they'll come along and we'll have to leave. And we won't be able to sleep in the Bedding Department and you won't be able to have the top bunk in the ship or the big doll for company.' So Angeline stopped crying so much and just sniffled a bit for appearance's sake, and then gave it up completely.

On we walked towards the Food Hall. We passed through the Flowers and then the Greengrocery sections on our way. The flowers were so lovely and so were all the displays of fresh fruit and vegetables. In fact everything in Scottley's was magnificent, including the rooms and the halls and the departments themselves, with their great high ceilings and their marble floors and with their huge wonderful chandeliers hanging down with hundreds of light bulbs on them, just like it was always Christmas.

And maybe it was too in Scottley's. That was the feeling it gave you: that it was always Christmas, that there was always something to celebrate and be excited about.

Little Angeline had taken Mum's hand by now, and as they walked along together she asked Mum a question I wouldn't have minded an honest answer to myself.

'Mum,' she said, 'will we be living in Scottley's long?'

'No, no,' Mum assured her, 'not long. Just till Monday, like I said.'

'But I want to live here long,' Angeline said. 'I like Scottley's'.

'Well, we'll have to see on Monday. We'll see if they have a flat for us yet, or maybe a little council house.'

'But Mum,' Angeline went on, 'what if it's Southfield again?'

Southfield is this part of the city with a terrible reputation for crime and drugs and all sorts of bad things.

'No,' Mum said, 'we're not going to Southfield. We'll sleep on the park bench before we go to Southfield.'

'But what if Southfield's all they've got?' little

Angeline persisted. 'Does that mean we'll be able to live in Scottley's forever? Is there a school that Livvy can go to in Scottley's? And is there a nursery for me?'

'We'll just have to see,' Mum told her, 'on Monday'.

My heart sank to the bottom of my boots when I heard her say that. Because much as Angeline wanted to live in Scottley's forever and a day, all I wanted to do was to get out of the place as soon as we could – as lovely and as cosy as it was. Because I could see that if anyone caught us there (and how could they *not* catch us, sooner or later?) we were going to get into the most awful trouble. And Mum would get into the biggest trouble of all, as she was supposed to be in charge. And if people didn't think that she was looking after us properly (and I knew a lot of people *would* think it and see things that way) then they might split us up, and send me and Angeline away and not let Mum be with us any more. And that was my worst nightmare. I dreaded that more than anything. I'd rather live on a park bench too, than let that happen. I didn't care if we had nothing else, just as long as we had each other.

As we passed through the Greengrocery

Department and headed for the Food Hall, I started to wonder just what we were going to get to eat. I mean, if we couldn't eat the chocolates in the Chocolate Department because we couldn't pay for them, how could we eat the food from the Food Hall? Because I was pretty sure that we didn't have the money to pay for any of that either. I didn't like to ask Mum though, as questions about how we were going to pay for things always annoyed her. So I just kept quiet and decided to wait and see.

The Food Hall was as beautiful as any of the other departments. It was almost as big as a church, with lines of food-laden shelves instead of lines of pews, and there was a great big cold meats counter the size of a church organ.

It wasn't simply any old stuff on display either, not like in some ordinary supermarket in the High Street. The shelves were full of all sorts of delicacies – some of which sounded quite horrible to me. There were tins of bulls' tongues in jelly and jars of pickled walnuts and there were all sorts of things with weird-sounding names. I found this horrible-looking black stuff in big jars in the cold cabinet. It was all lumpy and Mum said it was called caviare. And when you looked at the price ticket, it was about a hundred pounds for a jar of it. *A hundred pounds*. Just for black lumpy stuff that looked horrible and probably tasted even worse.

In another corner of the Food Hall there was this big sort of goldfish tank. Only when you went and looked inside, it wasn't goldfish that were in there, it was crabs – real live crabs and lobsters, dozens of them, all crawling over each other. When I asked Mum why the crabs were in the Food Hall and not in the Pets Department, she said that they weren't sold as pets, as generally speaking people don't get fond of crabs. No, she said that they were sold to be eaten and you were supposed to take them home and drop them in boiling water to kill them off.

I thought that was the most horrible thing I'd ever heard of, dropping live crabs into boiling water. I went right off Scottley's then and I silently swore that when I grew up I would come back to Scottley's and I would set all the crabs free. I'd somehow take them all down to the seaside and let them back into the ocean. And I'd be known as the 'Friend of the Crabs', or 'Super Livvy, the Lobster Liberator Lady'. And even if one of them bit me by accident and it hurt, I wouldn't be upset, as it would only be doing what came naturally.

And I'd forgive it just the same and say, 'Go, you poor creature. I don't blame you. Not even if you have bitten my arm off at the elbow. Have no fear. I have super powers and I'll soon grow another one.'

When I turned round from looking at the crabs, I saw that Mum had picked up a wire basket and she was over at the cold cabinet with Angeline and they were going through the ready-prepared meals together – the ones you only have to put in the microwave to warm up.

'See if you can find any with today's date,' Mum said. 'Any that say *Eat by 7th September*.'

I went over to help them. Well, to help Angeline, who isn't all that good at reading and dates, not yet.

We found several things that had to be sold by the seventh, and Mum read out what they were and we chose this meal called Fish Pie With Broccoli – Family Size. It wasn't that either Angeline or I were very keen on broccoli, but it was better than cabbage, which seemed to be in most of the other options.

'Okay,' Mum said, 'it's the seventh today and this pie hasn't been sold. That means that it will only be thrown away on Monday when the shop re-opens, because Monday will be the ninth, and by then it will be too late. So it's all right for us to eat it and in the circumstances that isn't stealing. If anything, it's just us being helpful, because it needs eating and we're doing it a favour in many ways and stopping good food from being wasted.'

Well, I didn't know if that was right or not. Maybe it was, maybe it wasn't. On balance, I think that Mum was probably right and I don't think it was stealing. I think that the food would have been thrown away if we hadn't eaten it and so we did the right thing. And it wasn't as if it had gone off. It was still fresh.

'But Mum,' Angeline said, 'it's cold. We can't eat cold fish pie with cold broccoli. That's too *eeech* for words. And we've got no plates and no knives and forks and no cups and saucers and no—'

'Don't worry,' Mum said, 'I've already thought of that. But first, see if there's anything for pudding that needs to be eaten today too and if there's anything to drink.'

So we had another look through the cold cabinets and we found a big carton of vanilla yoghurt and a litre of semi-skimmed milk, both of which had to be sold by the seventh.

'Okay,' Mum said, 'that'll do. Both carry something and follow me.'

So Mum took the fish pie, I took the yoghurt, Angeline took the milk, and off we went down the escalator to the basement, to Lamps and Bulbs, Kitchen Utensils and Domestic Appliances.

It was darker down in the basement, as there was no outside light coming in through the windows. It wasn't pitch-dark though and you could easily make out the lines of washing machines and deepfreezes and tumble-driers and dishwashers, all standing there like square snowmen, while the glow of the emergency exit lights gave them a tinge of red.

Mum picked up a torch from a display counter and turned it on. She found a light switch and flicked it and a couple of big standard lamps lit up.

'That's better,' she said. 'Follow me.' So we followed her across the basement, past the kettles and fridges and all the rest until finally we came to a display of microwave ovens.

'Right,' Mum said, 'now let's have a look,' and she went and had a look around the back of them until she found one that was plugged in. 'Okay,' she said, 'this will do.' Then she took the lid off the fish pie with broccoli, put the pie into the microwave and turned the oven on.

'Right,' she said. 'Let's get some plates.'

Off she went to the crockery and cutlery display, returned with three plates marked *Seconds – Reduced For Quick Sale*, three bowls marked *Party Plastic Range – Discontinued*, three sets of knives and forks which didn't match each other, plus a serving spoon and some teaspoons with slightly chipped handles from the Odds and Ends basket.

She set the plates, bowls and cutlery out on a kitchen table marked *Stainless Magi-Plast Non-Scratch Surface, One-Wipe Clean*, pulled up three chairs, and placed a cork mat in the middle of the table. Then, when the microwave oven pinged to let us know that the fish pie was piping hot, Mum borrowed a pair of oven gloves from the rack marked *Double Quilty Oven Gloves For Extra Safety*. She put them on, took out the foil tray and placed it on the cork *No Burn, No Scorch, No Tears, No Tantrums* table mat. Then, being careful not to spill any of the Fish Pie With Broccoli on to the table, she served up three helpings with the serving spoon – small, medium and large, just like for the three bears; only this time it was large for her, medium for me, and small for little Angeline.

We sat there, looking at the steaming fish pie. We were so hungry that even the broccoli smelt good – and that's saying something. It wasn't just fish and broccoli either, there were mashed potatoes in there and garden peas, and I realised as I watched the steam rise up and smelt that warm pie smell that I was absolutely my-throat's-been-cut starving.

'Can we start?' Angeline asked.

'Hold on,' Mum said, 'we need some glasses for the milk.'

Off she went again looking around the basement at the displays of kitchenware, to return with three plastic tumblers which she said were guaranteed unbreakable – but we weren't to try breaking them though, just in case they weren't.

Now, I noticed that all the stuff Mum was using was either scratch-proof or spot-proof or child-proof or wipeable or unbreakable, because plainly she wanted to wash everything up when we had finished with it and to put it all back on display, as good as new.

Well, I dare say she thought that she was being pretty clever too. And she did look rather pleased with herself, as we all sat there drinking our cold milk and munching away at our hot fish pie. It was almost as if she thought she'd been really inventive, thinking to find a microwave oven in the Kitchen Utensils and Domestic Appliances Department and then going round getting plates and knives and forks and all the rest. You'd have thought, to be honest, that she'd done us a tremendous favour and that she was being the best mum in the world – not that I'm saying she isn't the best mum in the world – by bringing us to live in Scottley's department store and eat warmed-up meals in the basement.

I mean, most mums would have been horrified. I can tell you are a bit too, just from looking at you. Especially that lady over there in the corner, the one who keeps tut-tutting all the time and who said she was a social worker.

Mum was certainly looking after us in her way though, that was true, and we weren't going short of anything. We did have a roof over our heads and nice warm beds to sleep in, and there was definitely no shortage of toys. But it was like we were mice, living in someone else's house. Yes, I felt that we were sort of living behind the skirting boards, picking up all the crumbs and the things that had been dropped or which weren't wanted. Yes, that was it, really, I felt she'd turned us into mice. Scottley's was this great big mansion and we were three little mice in it. Mum was Mrs Tittlemouse and we were her two daughters, Livvy Tittlemouse and little Angeline Tittlemouse, and there we were, all tittlemousing away in the basement, having Fish Pie With Broccoli.

But I didn't feel that turning us into mice was anything to be proud of. And if Mum imagined that she was being really clever, thinking of using the microwave in the Domestic Appliances Department, well, I reckoned that I had thought of something cleverer still. But I didn't know if I wanted to tell her about it, as I didn't really want to encourage her.

But then, as we all chewed away and when Mum said, 'Well girls? What do you think? Have I done you proud this time or haven't I?' I got so annoyed with her being so pleased with herself that I just had to say, 'Well, no, I don't think you have actually, Mum, to be honest.'

She gave me one of her looks then.

'Oh?' she said. 'Is that so, Miss? And in what way would you have done things better then, Olivia?'

I knew I'd annoyed her then, because she only ever calls me Miss and Olivia when she's fed up with me. The rest of the time it's Livvy. In fact I don't understand why she ever had me christened Olivia, because what use is a name if you're only going to use it when you're annoyed with someone?

'Well, Mum,' I said, 'it's *all right* eating down here and warming our dinner up in the Domestic Appliances section, but it's not *that* good, is it? Or that convenient.'

'And why not?' she said.

'Well,' I began, 'first we have to wash-up, and where are we going to do *that*?'

'I've already thought of that, Olivia,' she said. 'We'll wash-up the plates and so on in the ladies' loos.'

'Yes,' I nodded, 'that's what I thought you were going to say. Only the ladies' loos are back upstairs, aren't they? So we're going to have to carry everything up there to wash it and then carry it all the way back down here again. And then we'll have to make sure that it's all properly dry and nothing's damaged and that everything's put back exactly as it was.'

'So? What else could we do?'

'We could be eating our dinner,' I said, 'in the *cafeteria*.'

Mum narrowed her eyes then and gave me another of her looks. But she could see that I was right. There'd be plates in the cafeteria, and knives and forks and spoons and cups and tumblers, and sinks for washing-up and tea towels for drying and ovens for warming-up, and tomato ketchup too, probably, for shaking all over everything. And we wouldn't have had all this trouble of carrying things up to the ladies' loos.

'Hmm,' Mum said. 'I'll think about it.'

'Think about what?' Angeline asked.

'Eat your pie,' Mum said. 'And drink your milk while you're at it.'

But I knew she knew that I was right.

CHAPTER SIX

There isn't just one cafeteria in Scottley's either, there are loads. There's a proper restaurant with waiters and waitresses up on the very top floor, then there's a snack bar for children, situated right next to the Toy Department, called Planet Snacks. Then there's the ice-cream parlour, then there's the self-service canteen and the pizza parlour and the health food bar, and of course the coffee shop where they do drinks and pastries. Then there's something called a Tapas Bar, where they sell Spanish food, and something else called a Sushi Bar, where they serve Japanese delicacies and raw fish. And we knew that somewhere or other there must be a staff canteen.

We didn't know where the staff canteen was precisely, but we knew it couldn't be too far away. It must have lain beyond one of the many doors marked *Private, Staff Only*. I got the urge to go exploring every time I saw one of those *Staff Only* notices. I wanted to peep behind the scenes, to look past all the doors marked *Private* and *No Entry* and *No Customers Beyond This Point*. I didn't tell Mum though, she'd only have forbidden it. But as long as I didn't mention it, it would mean that she *hadn't* forbidden it, which meant that I could do it, as no one had said not to.

Only when would I get the chance?

Mum helped Angeline with the last of her fish pie, then she spooned out the vanilla yoghurt into the three bowls and we finished that as well. When that was done we drank the last of the milk and then we carried all the dishes up to the ladies' loo on the first floor where we washed everything in the sink, dried it under the hand-drier and took it all back to the basement. Mum brought some loo roll with her and used it to wipe the table and to make sure that everything was spotless. Then we put everything we had used back into its proper place.

Finally it was all done. We took the empty milk and yoghurt cartons, together with the packaging from the fish pie, and Mum tied the rubbish up inside a Scottley's carrier bag and dropped it into a bin. There were litter bins all over Scottley's, in all the departments. It was a very neat and tidy shop indeed.

Then we went back up to the Bedding Department. And felt at a bit of a loose end.

It was about half past seven by then and normally we'd have been having baths. In fact, Angeline would have been in bed. But as it was a Saturday and as it was all so exciting – us spending the night in Scottley's and everything – going to sleep was out of the question. To tell the truth, something got into us, and while Mum looked for our pyjamas in the big suitcase, Angeline and I went a bit mad. The urge suddenly came over us to run up and down the aisles of the Bedding Department, to scamper all the way through Soft Furnishings and right into Rugs, Mats and Floor Coverings. Then we hurled ourselves on top of this huge great pile of carpets and rolled around on them, doing cartwheels and handstands until Mum shouted at us to pack it in or there'd be big trouble. So we stopped that and began sliding down the banisters on the escalator instead, until Mum yelled at us to pack that in too as not only was it silly, it was dangerous.

'Come and put your pyjamas on!' she said. 'And

stop running about. It's not a playground, you know. It's a shop!'

But it was a playground. It was really. It was the biggest, greatest indoor playground in the world. I'd rather go back to Scottley's again than go to Disney Land or anywhere. But only if I could go with a few friends and we could have the whole place to ourselves. You see, there's something magic about Scottley's, there really is. To have that enormous store to run about in, with all those things to look at. It's the most magic place I've ever been in. Especially at night. You'd think it might be spooky, and maybe it is in places; but it's nice spooky, not really scary spooky. It's the best place in the whole world, and though I was against going there at first, I could really have stayed forever.

Mum laid our pyjamas out on the big four-poster bed.

'You ought to have baths really,' she said. 'Or at least wash your faces and hands. And you certainly must brush your teeth. We'd better go back to the ladies'.'

'Hang on, Mum,' I said (because I was desperate to waste time and not to go to bed for ages if I could possibly avoid it). 'Maybe we ought to go and have a look in the Bathrooms Department and see if any of the baths are working.'

She gave me one of her looks.

'Livvy,' she said, 'I think you know as well as I do that the baths in the Bathroom Department are not joined up to any hot water, nor are their plug-holes connected up to any drains either, come to that. They're just for show. You don't have demonstration bathtubs, like you have demonstration ovens or TVs, do you? When you buy a bath, you don't expect to try it out in the shop first, do you, and sit there with nothing on while all the other customers walk by?'

'No,' I agreed. But I hadn't given up. 'But you never know, Mum, there might be *one* that's working. And we've got our own towels, it's not as if we'd be using theirs, and we've got our own soap. So it might be worth having a *little* look . . . don't you think?'

Well, to be honest, I think that Mum wanted to go exploring around Scottley's just as much as little Angeline and I did. I think she also might have liked to go running through Soft Furnishings too, and then dive on to the big pile of carpets in Rugs, Mats and Floor Coverings, just the same as we did. Only she had to be grown-up and in charge so as to set us a good example. But she did want to go exploring, you could tell.

'Very well,' she said. 'I suppose we could go and have a look in the Baths and Showers section. Just for a minute. Here – you two carry your own towels – and I'll take your sponge bags.'

Well, we both had our pyjamas on by then and little Angeline had on her big fluffy slippers with the elephants' trunks at the front. So we took our towels and off we went, all the way back down to the basement where the baths and showers were situated, on the far side of Domestic Appliances. We trailed behind Mum like a couple of ducklings following a mother duck. And there was something so sort of warm and comforting about walking through Scottley's in your pyjamas and slippers that you just wanted to laugh out loud or to explode in bursts of giggles.

'And what are you two laughing at, might I ask?' Mum turned and asked as we headed down the escalator, trying to put on one of her stern faces and not really succeeding too well.

But we said we didn't know what we were laughing at and that we weren't really laughing anyway. And Angeline said it wasn't her, it was me. And normally I'd have said it wasn't and she was telling fibs. But not that night. I didn't want to argue. Being in Scottley's in your slippers and pyjamas with your bath towel in your arms just made you want to pick up the nearest person and give them a good long squeeze. So that was what I did. I picked up little Angeline and gave her a good long squeeze. And we didn't quarrel for ages after that, not for almost half an hour.

So back down we went. We were really getting to know our way around now and we were soon back in the gloomy basement. Mum put some lights on and over we went to inspect Baths and Showers.

Well, it was just as Mum had suspected. None of the baths were plumbed in at all. They were all there for show, not for filling up with water.

Angeline and I got into one of them anyway, just for a bit of fun. We had pretend baths in this enormous tub which was practically as big as a swimming pool, but without the diving boards.

'You'd need to be a rich person with a very big house to afford a bath like that,' Mum said solemnly, just as if she knew a lot of rich people and had spent a lot of time with them talking about their bath problems. 'It's not just the cost of filling it with hot water, it's having the space.'

And she was right there. Because that bath was nearly as big as the last flat we had stayed in. And it seemed very odd to me that our old home was no bigger than someone else's bath tub. Very odd indeed.

They did have some lovely baths there though. They had them with gold taps and even with gold plugs sitting in golden plug holes with gold chains attached to them – just like the necklaces ladies wear. There were baths with taps shaped like dolphins. There were round baths, half-circle baths, and old-fashioned style baths from years ago. There were things called whirlpool baths, and wave baths which had warm currents of water in them when you turned them on and they would bubble away, Mum said, just like a kettle on a stove.

Anyway, we sat in the baths and admired them a while and then we all chose the one we would have if we were rich and in a big house and could have a bath each. But we didn't get any washing done as there wasn't any water. So finally Mum said, 'Okay, girls, that's enough now. We'll have to sort something out tomorrow. Let's just go to the ladies' and brush your teeth and then it'll be time for bed.'

Well, you could tell she meant it and there was no point in arguing, so we followed her out of Baths and Showers, turned off the lights, and went back up to the ground floor.

'This way,' Mum said. 'We'll try the stairs this time.'

So we followed her up the proper stairs to the next floor, instead of using the escalator as we had done so far. And it was a lucky thing we did too, because when we came to the first landing, I saw a door with a sign on it saying *Staff Only*. And I had an idea.

'Mum,' I said, 'you know these *Staff Only* doors . . .'

'Yes?' she said, rather suspiciously.

'Well,' I said, 'I bet the staff canteen must be down there somewhere, behind one of those *Staff Only* doors, don't you think?'

'Possibly,' she nodded, still a bit wary. 'Why?'

'Well,' I said, 'I bet it's not just a staff canteen they have. I bet in a big place like this they'd also have special cloakrooms for the staff, you know, staff ladies' and staff gentlemen's, and possibly even – staff showers?'

'Yes, Mum,' little Angeline chipped in, 'and maybe even a staff bouncy castle.'

'Well, perhaps,' Mum agreed, looking a bit doubtful.

'Can we go and have a look then?' I said.

'Okay,' she grinned. 'Let's go. Or at least we'd better see if the door's locked first.'

But it wasn't. So she pushed it open and there we were, in the private and personal special corridor where only the staff could go. There were things there that the customers never got to see; and we were about to see them, we were about to get a peek behind the scenes.

So we ran up after Mum and took a hand each, and on we went, into the unknown.

It was colder and darker than in the store itself. There was still enough light though to see where you were going. There were the usual, red-glowing emergency exit signs, supplemented by pale white moonlight and the yellow glow of the city outside, coming in through the corridor windows.

It wasn't all that nice there though. No deep, thick, warm, luxurious carpets on that corridor. Just cold, clattering concrete. Mum's shoe heels click-clacked over it and our slippers went scuff-scuff-scuff.

It didn't smell so sweet either. There was no aroma of perfume, more of bathroom cleaner or that stuff you pour down toilets. It was draughty too, and the walls seemed to be painted a nasty green, as far as I could make out in the gloom.

It was all a bit of a disappointment. It was like seeing behind the scenes of a theatre, which we'd done once on a school trip. It was like finding out how a conjuring trick was done. It took all the magic away. Well, not *all* of it and only for a while. Once we were back in the shop itself, the magic immediately returned. But whenever we went beyond one of the doors marked *Staff Only* – which we did quite frequently – the wonder of the store just vanished and you were back into the ordinary world. It gave me the same kind of feeling as I used to get when we went to the cinema, when the film was over and it was time to go. And you had to leave the fantasy behind you and walk out into the cold, damp, gloomy world, buttoning up your coat as you went.

Anyway, we went along the *Staff Only* corridor until we came to a set of swing doors. We pushed our way through them and marched on a little further to where the corridor divided into two. One direction lead to the *Staff Canteen and Executive*

Restaurant (so the signs on the wall said) and the other way was illuminated with a picture of a lady, a picture of a man (like you get outside public toilets) and lastly a picture of a shower-head with water coming out.

'Ah, ha!' Mum said. 'Here we are. Looks like we won't be going to bed unwashed after all.' So on we went, a bit further down the corridor, until we came to a door with another shower-head picture on it and the word 'shower' written underneath, so there could be no confusion, and in we went.

And there they were, three shower cubicles, all in a line. Very spick and span they were too. And when Mum turned the water on, it was piping hot. So hot, she had to turn it down a bit before she'd let us get under. And the water really poured down too, just like a waterfall.

'This is good, isn't it,' Mum said as she watched us get clean. 'It's certainly the best hotel I've ever stayed in.' Which was a sort of joke of hers really, as we'd never stayed in any hotels. But we knew what she meant and so we laughed anyway and we said it was the best hotel we had ever stayed in too.

Now when you got into the showers, there were these bottles there of complimentary shampoo and complimentary shower gel. Mum said 'complimentary' meant that you could help yourself to as much as you wanted, as long as you weren't greedy and didn't go mad. So me and Angeline decided that we might as well wash our hair then, which we did. And this time little Angeline actually managed to do it without getting soap in her eyes and without standing there yelling for half an hour, going, 'Towel, towel, towel!' even when you'd given her about twenty towels already.

Well, I can tell you, it was really good stuff that shower gel. Expensive too, I reckon. It was Scottley's own make, which just tells you how good it was. And when we showed it to Mum, she said, 'You know, I wouldn't mind having a shower myself,' and so she did too. And we didn't half all smell lovely by the time we'd finished. I wish you could have smelt us really, we smelt that nice. I think it was probably the best we'd ever smelled in our lives. I shouldn't think I'll ever smell that nice again, not even if I live to be a hundred.

They even had free hairdryers in the staff shower room, so we all got to dry our hair. Then I saw that there was complimentary talcum powder and complementary eau de cologne (which is a sort of perfume for splashing all over yourself) and there was some complimentary moisturising body cream on offer too. So we all had a few dabs of all that stuff too. Then we all brushed our teeth and then finally we were done.

We helped Mum tidy up the shower room before we went, and we left it behind us as clean as when we had found it – cleaner, if anything – and nobody would ever have known we had been there.

So then it was back along the corridor. On our way we took a quick peek in through the doors of the big staff canteen. It was huge and echoey and when you said, 'Hello,' your voice said 'hello' back to you, two or three times over, and then it vanished behind the counter.

'Come on then,' Mum said. 'Bedtime. Now we know where the canteen is, we can come back for breakfast in the morning.'

So we went back down the corridor and into the store and then up to our beds in the Bedding Department.

It must have been really late by then – well, really late for Angeline. It had certainly gone nine o'clock. She climbed up the ladder to the top 'cabin' in the ship-shaped bunk bed, got in beside the great big all-singing, dancing, crying and knicker-wetting doll she had borrowed from the Toy Department, and Mum and I both kissed her goodnight. Then we had to kiss the doll goodnight too, to keep Angeline happy, and within minutes she was asleep. But funnily enough, the doll's eyes popped open, just as Angeline dozed off. And it did look funny, little Angeline fast asleep, and the doll wide awake. Just like it was watching over her. Just like it was her big sister and not me.

Well, once Angeline fell asleep, Mum sort of collapsed on to the big four-poster bed, and she looked really tired. I knew it was a strain for her and I knew why, because it was a big strain for me too. It was all the pretending, that's what did it. While little Angeline was awake I had to pretend that it was all a great lark and a big game and loads of fun. I had to carry on as if sleeping in Scottley's was the next best thing to being on your holidays. But it wasn't at all. And I knew it wasn't. I knew why we were sleeping in Scottley's – and we weren't doing it for a laugh. We were doing it because we had to, because we had nowhere else to go – at least nowhere else that Mum *would* go. The truth was that we were homeless.

* * *

I went and sat on the bed next to Mum and waited until she opened her eyes.

'Mum,' I said. 'How long are we going to stay in Scottley's for?'

'Just till Monday,' she said. 'Two nights, that's all. It's just for the weekend. Then, first thing on Monday, we'll go to the Housing Office and see if they've got anywhere that we can go. Don't worry, Livvy, it'll be all right.'

'But Mum,' I said, though I could tell that she'd rather I kept quiet and didn't go on about it, 'but Mum, what if they only have a flat in Southfield again?'

She sat up on the bed.

'We are not,' she said, 'ever going to live in Southfield. *Ever*. I am not having my children growing up in a place like that.'

'But what if that's all they have for us, Mum? What then?'

'Then we'll just have to see, Livvy, we'll just have to see.'

And that was what she always said. Whenever I asked her any difficult questions, it was always the same answer, 'We'll just have to see, Livvy, we'll just have to wait and see.'

Only I hate it when people go on about having to wait and see. I need to know. To know *now*! I need to know, to put my mind at rest. But with Mum, we never did see. It was all wait and no see at all. That was what I didn't like.

Mum closed her eyes again.

'Mum,' I said, 'how's Dad going to send us letters if we're living in Scottley's?'

'They'll keep them for us at the post office, Livvy. And we're not living here. We're just lodging here for two days at the most, that's all.'

And she closed her eyes once more.

'Mum—'

'What now, Livvy?'

'What if someone finds us?'

'Who's going to find us?'

'Someone might.'

'Who?'

'Mr Whiskers.'

'Who's Mr Whiskers?'

'You know, the doorman. Scottley's doorman. Him.'

'Well, he won't come in, will he? Not if he's the doorman. He stays by the door. And he won't be here now anyhow. It's the weekend. He'll be at home doing ... whatever doormen do at the weekend.'

I had a sudden vision then of Mr Whiskers standing in the doorway of his own house, saying hello and goodbye to his family as they went in and out.

'Thank you for your custom, Mum,' he'd say. 'Thank you for shopping at Whisker's.'

'That's all right son. The pleasure's mine. Can you just whistle up a taxi for me? Or better still, whistle up a bus. A taxi's a bit expensive ...'

'But Mum –' I said, poking Mum in the ribs to stop her falling asleep.

'What now, Livvy?'

'What if a night-watchman or somebody comes round. Or a security patrol?'

'I'm sure it'll be all right.'

'But what if they *do* and they find us here?'

'Well, we'll deal with that when it happens.'

'But I'm worried, Mum.'

'Then you have to stop being worried. There's always things to worry about. Livvy. You just mustn't let yourself worry about them so much, or you'll never be happy.'

'But Mum, there's another thing too. How do we get out?'

'What do you mean?'

'How do we get out of the shop on Monday morning? They'll find us here, won't they?'

'No, we'll hide somewhere and sneak out as soon as the doors are opened.'

'But what if we sleep in? Our alarm clock doesn't work very well. It's not reliable. If you set it to ring at seven it doesn't go off till ten.'

'Then we'll borrow one tomorrow, just for the night, from the Clocks and Watches Department.'

'But Mum—'

'It'll be all right, Livvy. Don't worry. Just try and enjoy it while you can. Thousands of children would love to spend the night sleeping in the Bedding Department in Scottley's. They'd love to change places with you.'

Yes, I thought, *and they've all got proper homes and houses. I'd love to change places with* them.

'Come on, Livvy, you're such a tower of strength. I'd never have managed without you. And little Angeline, she just follows you everywhere.'

'I'm not, Mum. I'm not a tower of strength.'

'You are to me,' she said.

Well, maybe. But I wasn't to myself. I was a tower of quivering jelly as far as I was concerned.

'Okay, I'll try not to worry for a while. But I'm

sure I'll only begin worrying again, first thing in the morning.'

'Well, at least you'll have had a good night's sleep.'

'Mum, I even worry in my sleep sometimes.'

'I know. And that's why we're going to find a real home for us, somewhere we'll never have to move from, ever. And then you won't have to worry again, Livvy, except about little things.'

'Okay, Mum. Only *when* will we find somewhere? And when's Dad coming home from the oil wells? Because I don't remember him at all. It seems like I've never even met him sometimes. I do have a dad, don't I?'

'Of course you do, Livvy.'

'When will he be coming home then?'

'We'll just have to wait and see. Try and get to sleep now.'

'Okay. 'Night, Mum.'

''Night.'

So we had a kiss and a cuddle and I got into the bottom bunk of the ship-shaped bunk bed and Mum turned off the big standard lamp and I soon fell asleep, despite my worries. I think that I must have slept for a good two or three hours before I woke. But when I did wake, it was to worry even more than ever.

No, it wasn't that anyone had disappeared. Mum was still there – fast asleep on the big, double, four-poster bed – and Angeline was gurgling away above me.

The reason I was worried – the reason I was afraid – was that there was someone else there. There was somebody else in the Bedding Department. And he was heading our way.

CHAPTER SEVEN

It was a watchman, or a security guard, or whatever you care to call them. He was wearing a uniform and carrying a big heavy torch, which he shone around the department as he strolled slowly along the aisle.

I didn't know where he had come from or how he had got in. Maybe he'd just arrived in a van which he'd left parked outside and he'd let himself into Scottley's with a set of keys in order to make his nightly patrol.

Was he on his own, I wondered, or was there someone with him, maybe patrolling one of the other floors at that very moment?

Then I thought of something awful. What if he'd been there *all along*? What if he'd been in Scottley's all the time we'd been cooking fish pie and having showers and playing in the Toy Department? What if he'd been there walking around or sitting in a

102

little office somewhere and we hadn't known? He might have heard us. He might have run into us at any moment. It didn't bear thinking about. He might have walked round the corner and there we'd have been, getting stuck into Fish Pie With Broccoli, with vanilla yoghurt for afters. And even if the fish pie had been past its sell-by date, I don't think that would have impressed him too much.

And what now? What if he discovered us, tucked up in our beds? And he couldn't *not* see us. Not if he came along our aisle. It would lead him right past the bunk bed and the four-poster. And if he didn't see us he'd probably hear us, especially if Mum started snoring or if little Angeline had one of her gurgling fits. She could gurgle really loudly sometimes, sounding just like the last bit of milk in a glass when you slurped it up the straw. And Mum wasn't bad on the snoring either. When she got started it was like somebody blasting rocks in a quarry.

They were both fairly quiet at the moment, but if the watchman came much closer he was bound to hear them, *bound* to. The store was so quiet too; just the drone of the traffic outside behind the thick, double-glazed windows and the hum of the heating system. Those background noises were so faint I could actually hear the watchman's footsteps, muffled as they were by the thick, deep carpet. And if I could hear him, then surely he could hear little Angeline – even if she was gurgling very quietly.

Or maybe his hearing wasn't as good as mine. Your hearing isn't as sharp when you get older. Maybe he'd be really old and not hear her at all. But then he couldn't be *that* old, or he wouldn't be a security man. Because you can't go running after robbers and shouting, 'Stop that man, he's a burglar!' – not when you're really old, not with any hope of catching them.

Maybe he was just a little bit old. That would be something.

I could make him out now. I saw the torch flashing around the department. He was about a hundred metres away and getting nearer. He suddenly began to whistle. The shrill, sharp noise nearly made me jump up and bang my head on the bottom of Angeline's bunk. But I soon recovered. *Go on*, I thought, *go on, keep whistling, make all the noise you can. Make so much noise that you won't hear Angeline gurgling, not even if you walk right by her*.

He came to a junction where two aisles crossed.

If he kept going straight on, we were done for. If he turned left or right, we were okay.

I waited.

He waited.

He waited even longer.

He just stood there whistling, as if he couldn't make up his mind which way to go. Then I heard a voice. It must have been coming from the radio on his belt. It was all squawky and said nothing I could understand, but the man spoke back into it saying, 'Bravo One here, nearly finished at Scottley's. Time now twelve forty-five. Estimate another fifteen minutes here, then on to the next call. Over and out.'

Well, that was all very useful to know. But me knowing it on my own wasn't going to be enough. I needed someone else to see this. I needed to wake Mum up.

Now, I knew that this was a big risk, and I know you'll probably think I was stupid to have taken it. But that's because you don't know our mum. You see, if I'd just woken next morning and said, 'Mum, there was a watchman patrolling the Bedding Department last night and he nearly caught us in our pyjamas,' she'd either have thought that I'd dreamt it up or she simply wouldn't have been that bothered.

See, I'm the worrier in our family. Every family has a worrier and in my family it happens to be me. Now it maybe is true that I do worry too much. But our mum doesn't worry enough. In fact she hardly worries at all. Getting Mum to worry is like trying to pump up a bicycle tyre with a puncture in it. You're fighting a losing battle.

I mean, you have to do a bit of worrying sometimes, don't you, or you'd take all kinds of stupid risks. You'd jump out of aeroplanes with no parachute, and when people said it was dangerous, you'd just say, 'No, it's nothing to worry about. I'll probably land in a pond or on a haystack or on something squashy in a jelly factory, I'll be all right.'

Well, our mum can be a bit like that sometimes and I knew that if I wanted her to take this night watchman seriously, she'd have to be woken up to see him for herself. And that was very risky indeed. Because the first thing our mum does when she wakes up is to stretch and let out a big long, loud, 'Ahhhhhh!' And I didn't want any big, long, loud *Ahhhhhh*s! I can tell you. Not me. So I had to wake her up and stop her going *Ahhhhhh!* at the same time. Which meant I had to get out of the bunk bed without making a noise, crawl over to the four-poster, get my hand over Mum's mouth to stop the *Ahhhhh*! and then give her a poke to wake her up.

And all this without the man seeing me.

Go! I told myself. *Go!*

And I did. I rolled silently out of the bunk bed and on to the thick, deep carpet. I rolled over a few more times, right under the four-poster bed and then up at the other side. I knelt up, got a hand over Mum's mouth, and gave her a good hard wake-up-right-now poke in the ribs.

Her eyes opened immediately. I could feel her mouth opening too, all ready to go *Ahhhhh*! I tightened my grip. Her eyes saw me.

'Mum,' I whispered into her ear. 'There's someone in here.'

I looked towards the man and her eyes followed mine. I took my hand off her mouth and raised my finger to my lips. She looked a bit panicky, as if she had started to worry at last. The two of us watched, waiting for the watchman to decide which way to go. Finally he made up his mind.

He walked towards us.

Oh no, I thought, *oh no, oh, no, oh no!*

But then his radio crackled again and he

stopped, listened, and then spoke into it. 'Okay, Tango,' he said, 'I'm just about done here anyway. I'll come directly down now.' And he turned and went back the way he had come, and we heard his footsteps going down the escalator.

And we were safe again. For a while.

Little Angeline went on gurgling. *It's all right for you*, I thought. *You don't have to worry. It's only me who does all that. And I don't just worry for myself, I have to worry for two others as well*. But it wasn't her fault she was little and didn't have to worry about things and had nothing better to do than gurgle. She looked a bit funny too, stuck up there in her bunk bed with a doll that was as big as she was and which still had its eyes open.

'Mum!' I hissed. 'What're we going to do?'

'It's all right, Livvy,' she whispered. 'He's gone now. We can get back to sleep.' And she lay back down on the pillow and closed her eyes.

Get back to *sleep*? I couldn't believe it. Get back to sleep *now*? After what had just happened? There was no way I could get back to sleep; I'd be up for the rest of the night. I'd be awake for the next two hundred years.

I returned to my bunk bed for a while and tried

to relax and to put my mind at rest. I counted more sheep than they have in Australia, but it was no good; I couldn't settle. So I clambered out of bed again and got in beside Mum in the big four-poster. She was lovely and warm and smelt of all that complimentary Scottley's shower gel and talc and what have you. What I wanted to do more than anything was to put my arms around her and for her to put her arms around me and tell me everything was going to be all right. But that was the problem. Mum's a bit too quick to tell you everything's going to be all right, especially when it's going to be all wrong. She's not really one to make what I think is known as 'provision for the future'. I had to give her a telling off.

She opened her eyes when she felt me getting in beside her.

'Hello, Livvy. You all right? Bad dream?'

'It's not a bad dream, Mum. It's a bad really-happening. That man! What if he comes back?'

'Oh, I shouldn't think he'll come back now, love. He probably just looks in once a night. I shouldn't think we'll see him again. We should be all right till morning.'

'But what if he *does* come back, Mum? What then?'

'Well, he didn't find us this time, so he might not the next.'

'But what if he *does*, Mum?'

'Well, I shouldn't think he will.'

'But what about tomorrow, Mum? What are we going to do for Sunday night? We can't stay here. Not in the Bedding Department. He'll find us. Or it might be another man next time. Or two of them. What are we going to do tomorrow?'

'Well, maybe they don't work on Sundays, Livvy.'

'But what if they *do*?'

'Well, we'll sort that out tomorrow, shall we? Night, night.'

'But Mum . . . Mum . . .'

But it was no good. She'd gone back to sleep. Just like that. Just like we were all warm and safe and cosy in our own little house and had nothing to worry about at all. I don't know how she managed it. I really don't. All I could do was lie there and feel sick.

I stayed in the four-poster, looking up at the ceiling of the Bedding Department. Then I looked around and started seeing things in the shadows. I kept thinking I saw flickerings and movements behind the wardrobes. I had to get out of bed in the end and go and have a look. I went dashing behind chests of drawers and vanity units going, 'Who is it?' and 'Who's there?' And I wasn't doing it because I was brave, I was doing it because I was terrified and it was easier to look than not to.

At last I calmed down and I went and got back in beside Mum in the big four-poster. I didn't want to go back to my own bunk as it would have got cold by now, and besides, I felt lonely.

I put my head on the pillow and stared at the ceiling again. Seeing as I'd already counted all the sheep in Australia, I decided to count all the tea pots in China this time and then – if I was still awake – to count all the lids as well. I got up to ten thousand and sixty something and then gradually my eyes felt heavy and my eyelids began to close and the last thing I remember hearing was little Angeline gurgling and Mum snoring.

As I drifted into sleep, I wondered what I'd ever done to be born into such a family, with a dad I'd hardly met, a mum who never worried much and who'd brought us to spend the weekend in Scottley's Bedding Department, and a little sister who gurgled all the time and who shared a bed

111

with a daft doll that was bigger than she was and which kept its eyes open all night and wet its knickers when you weren't looking.

I wondered if maybe I hadn't been adopted and if I didn't really belong somewhere else. Or maybe I'd been carried away by fairies when I was just a baby. Maybe I'd once lived in a big house with a large bath in it, just like the one down in Scottley's basement, and we'd had proper bedrooms and we didn't have men in security uniforms coming round disturbing you at quarter to one in the morning.

Yes, maybe that was it. Maybe I wasn't really part of this family at all. Maybe they'd escaped from a lunatic asylum and I'd just fallen in with them by mistake.

Only I knew I *was* part of it. I looked so like Mum, I had to be. And I heard Angeline gurgle and Mum snoring, and I sort of resented them both. And yet I loved them too and I knew they were all I had. I just wished it could have been different, that was all, and that we could be like other families; and that maybe I could meet my dad again one day, that he'd come home from the oil wells with loads of money, and we'd all live in a proper house, and be happy ever after, just like in the stories. That was what I wanted, more than anything.

And then at last I fell asleep.

CHAPTER EIGHT

The dawn woke us. There were no blinds or curtains on the store windows, so it got light inside as soon as the sun came up. Not that the sun rises all that early at this time of year, but I felt as if I'd been awake half the night and could have done with a long lie-in.

Little Angeline was first out of bed. I looked and there she was peering down at me, her huge doll standing next to her. Now that it was daytime, the doll's eyes were closed. It seemed to do everything the wrong way round.

'What are you doing in Mum's bed?' Angeline asked.

'Feeling exhausted,' I told her.

'Not fair,' she said. 'I want to feel exhausted too!'

But then things were never really fair as far as Angeline was concerned – not even when she had *more* than you. I remember her having a terrible fit once because she had more sweets than I did. That's right, *more*! She went absolutely bananas and stomped about all over the place going, 'Livvy's got less than I have. Not fair, not fair!'

And she wasn't happy until we had the same. And I'd thought I was being kind in giving her the larger share. But there you are, you can never tell with some people, especially sisters. They're only happy when they're miserable.

'You can come in with me tonight then if you want to,' Mum offered, trying to placate her.

'What about if the man comes round again?' I asked.

'What man?' Angeline demanded.

'Nobody,' Mum said. 'Now, does anybody need the bathroom?'

Well, we all did. So before we did anything else, we all had to troop off to the ladies'. And I must say that I did find that side of things very annoying. The ladies' was such a long way away it was a good ten minutes' walk there and back. It wasn't like at home where the bathroom's just up the stairs, it was more like it was out in the garden. And that really did make me fed-up, that part of it, that whenever you needed to use the toilet you

115

had to go off on an expedition.

To be honest, I think that Scottley's could have had a toilet a bit nearer to the Bedding Department for the convenience of their customers. And if they have a suggestions box – although I never noticed one – it might be worthwhile someone mentioning that.

Anyway, off we went to do our 'ablutions' as Mum called them and to wash our faces and hands and to brush our teeth again. Then we came back to the Bedding Department and started to get dressed. Mum took our dirty things and put them in a carrier bag which then went into the big suitcase.

'I hope we don't run out of clean clothes, Mum,' I said.

'Oh, we'll find some way of washing them, I'm sure,' Mum said. 'We'll worry about it later.' (Worry about it *later*, you see. Same old thing. It was just another way of not worrying about it at all.)

'I'm hungry,' Little Angeline said. 'What's for breakfast?'

'Let's go and see what we can find,' Mum said. So off we went, back down to the enormous Food Hall to see what we could get.

Well, we must have looked at practically every box of cereal on the shelves, searching for a packet that was past its sell-by date, but there wasn't a single one.

'Okay,' Mum said, getting a few coins out of her pocket, 'we'll have to buy one. What shall we have? Cornflakes?'

Cornflakes it was.

'How're you going to pay for them, Mum?' I asked. 'There's no one to take the money.'

'We'll have to leave it by the till,' she decided, and she went and did so, grumbling a bit about the price of cornflakes in Scottley's, saying how expensive they were and how you could get them a lot cheaper elsewhere. Which was probably true. But they were very good cornflakes, I will say that. You can always rely on Scottley's for quality.

Anyway, we were luckier with the milk. We found another litre bottle just past its sell-by date, but it still smelt fresh, and we found a loaf of bread too that was past its sell-by date as well. We couldn't find any butter and jam past their sell-by dates however, so Mum had to buy them as well, and soon there were three little piles of coins stacked up by the till.

They worried me.

'Mum,' I said, 'I know you're only being honest, paying for these things, but won't they think it strange when they come in on Monday morning to find three little heaps of money? Won't it make them ... well, suspicious? Make them start to wonder if someone hasn't been in here? When they weren't supposed to be.'

'Well, we've got to pay for the things, Livvy. Not to pay would be dishonest.'

'Well, can't we pay in another way, Mum? Can't we pay in a way that wouldn't make anyone suspicious, that they might not even notice?'

'Well, how?'

'We ... we could do some work, Mum,' I said. 'We could *work* for the cornflakes and the butter and jam.'

'Work? What kind of work?'

'Well, cleaning and tidying-up maybe.'

'But they'll have cleaners, Livvy. They must have cleaners in a place like this.'

'They don't always do a very good job then, because I've seen plenty of dust and spiders' webs in loads of places.'

'Yes, me too,' little Angeline chipped in. (Though she probably hadn't seen any at all.)

'So why don't we do what they've missed?' I suggested. 'We can work out what would be fair payment – so much an hour. And when we've done enough to pay for what we've taken, we can stop.'

'All right,' Mum said 'We'll do that.' And she took the coins back from next to the till. 'But we all have to pull our weight and do our share.'

'Of course.'

'All right then. Let's go and have our breakfast first.'

And so we took up the bread, the butter, the jam, the milk and the cornflakes, and off we headed up to the staff canteen.

As we pushed our way through the door marked *Staff Only*, another worry entered my head. It was what Mum had said about the cleaners. It was true. Of course there would be cleaners, a whole team of them for a place like this. But when were they going to arrive? And what were we going to do when they got there? They'd clean the whole store, wouldn't they, from top to bottom? They might not do it so well in places, but they did it after a fashion. So they'd be bound to find us, wouldn't they? *Bound* to. I mean, maybe one security guard you could hide from, but not a whole army of cleaners.

What were we going to do?

Mum went and got some bowls from the racks of plates in the staff canteen while I worried silently to myself. I'd have to talk to her about the cleaners, but not now, not during breakfast or in front of little Angeline. Later.

It was huge that staff canteen, as big as a railway station and it was a bit chilly too. But Mum let us go behind the counter with her and that was quite exciting, as I'd never been behind a counter before. We got our plates and knives and spoons and glasses sorted out and went and took them over to a table. First we had our cornflakes, then we all went back behind the counter to make the toast.

Now the toaster there was almost the size of a piano and it gleamed like polished silver and it could actually do *twelve* pieces of toast all at once. So we filled it right up, toasted twelve slices, put them on a plate, took them over to the table, and we wolfed the lot. And then we went and made another three bits as well. We were starving.

'I like living in Scottley's,' little Angeline said as she munched on her fifth slice of toast. 'Let's stay here forever.'

'Umm,' Mum agreed, 'let's do that.'

And I gave them both a filthy look.

We had the milk to drink. I wouldn't have minded some orange juice, as there was a whole tank of it on display by the counter. I didn't like to ask though. But I must have kept looking at it because finally Mum said, 'Did you want some juice, Livvy?'

'Well, I was just wondering,' I said, 'how much work you'd have to do for a glass of orange.'

'Yes,' Mum said. 'And I was just wondering how much work you'd have to do for a tea-bag. Because I can see some up there, and I'd love a cup of tea. *And* we've got the milk. Hmmm.'

'I reckon,' I said, 'that you'd have to do about ten minutes, cleaning and dusting for a tea-bag.'

'And I reckon,' Mum said, 'that orange juice would be about the same.'

'How about me?' Angeline said. 'Will I have to work for my orange juice too?'

'No,' I said. 'I'll buy this one for you. I'll do twenty minutes' work for two glasses of orange juice.'

'Thanks, Livvy,' she said. 'You're very kind. Even if you are a bit boring sometimes.'

So I fetched two glasses of juice and Mum got her tea-bag and went to boil up some water. She managed to get *two* cups of tea as well out of that tea-bag, which I thought was a bit unfair, because it meant she only had to do ten minutes for two drinks whereas I had to do twenty. But then I thought that she'd probably work off the cost of all our cornflakes as well, so I didn't complain.

When breakfast was over we washed all the dishes up and wiped all the surfaces down and went and put our food and things in the big fridge there. There was loads of stuff inside it and we put our belongings to one corner so as not to get them mixed up.

Once it was all done, you'd never have known that a soul had been in there. We left the place just as we had found it – only maybe a bit cleaner, that was all.

'Okay,' Mum said. 'Let's go and do a spot of cleaning and dusting then, to pay for those cornflakes and everything else.'

So that was what we did.

We didn't use any cleaning things from the Domestic Utensils Department as Mum said it would be wrong to go dirtying new dusters and using unopened tins of polish and so on. Instead we found a broom cupboard in the *Staff Only* corridor, situated right next to the shower room. There was lots of cleaning stuff in there: mops, brooms, feather dusters, the lot. We took what we needed and went off in search of dust and dirty bits – the bits that the usual cleaners had got into the habit of missing.

'I think,' Mum said, 'that we should begin right here. Because the shop part of the store is very well looked after, but it's not quite the same in the *Staff Only* section. So let's make a start on this corridor and the stairs. But be careful not to trip.'

So we got to work. I did some sweeping and polishing, while Mum went round with a vacuum cleaner she had found in the cupboard. The vacuum cleaner's name was Henry. I knew because it was written on him. I'd never met a vacuum cleaner with a name before.

Little Angeline went round with the feather duster, waving it about as if she was someone's fairy godmother. She still had that doll in tow too, though I kept reminding her that it wasn't hers to keep and that it would have to go back to the Toy Department. And she kept saying, 'I know, I know, you don't have to tell me!' But I knew she'd be upset when it was time to part with it.

Little Angeline wasn't really much use to be honest, she just spread the dust around more than anything. But she did try. And every minute or so she'd say, 'There. That's another cornflake paid for.' So her heart was in the right place. But she could certainly eat cornflakes a lot quicker than she could pay for them.

I think we were even starting to rather enjoy ourselves. It took your mind off your troubles, the cleaning did. It wasn't a difficult job, I mean not up in your brain, but it was nice to be doing something and you were moving about and keeping busy. You didn't have the time to worry.

We must have been working for almost an hour and by my calculations everything was pretty well paid for, cornflakes, jam and all the rest. But then, as I went round with the duster and polish, I heard a far sound, coming faintly over the drone of Henry the vacuum cleaner.

'Mum,' I said. 'Put Henry off a minute. I heard something.'

'What? What was it?'

'Have we paid for all the cornflakes yet?' Angeline asked, seeing that we had both stopped working.

'Shhh!' I said. 'Listen.'

There it was again. And there was no mistaking it now. It wasn't my imagination as I'd thought at first (because I'd got a bit jumpy after the night watchman had appeared, and I'd started hearing things everywhere). But no, there was no doubt about it, someone else was in the store. More than some*one*, too. It wasn't just one person on their own, there seemed to be loads of them.

'What're we going do?' I said. 'Where're we going to hide? Quick, come on, let's all get in the broom cupboard! Or lock ourselves in a toilet cubicle in the ladies'. Let's find a big one, one large enough for three, so we can all get in at once.'

'Livvy,' Mum said, 'stop expecting the worst for a moment. Don't panic immediately. First let's see what's going on.'

She left Henry the vacuum cleaner in the corridor, a pipe trailing out of his nose just like he was a little elephant, and hurried to an alcove where there was a big window looking down into the alleyway that ran along the side of the Scottley's building.

I grabbed little Angeline's hand and ran with her to join Mum and to see what was going on. When I peered down into the alley – keeping back a bit just in case somebody looked up and saw us – it was to see four or five vans with *Carter's Contract Cleaning Services* written on their roofs (and probably their sides too) and there was a whole gang of people out there, busily unloading cleaning equipment.

'The cleaners,' Mum whispered. 'It's the cleaners.'

'But *we're* the cleaners,' little Angeline said indignantly.

'The *real* cleaners!' I told her.

'Wanna see!' she said (because she hated to be left out of anything), so I had to lift her up so that she could peer down into the alleyway as well.

'Cor,' she said, 'lotsa people.'

But she didn't need to sound so pleased about it.

There was the drone of vacuum cleaners and floor polishers and carpet cleaners next. Some of the cleaning gang were already in the building and working away, even as the others unloaded the vans. It was hard to guess how many cleaners there were altogether. We could see at least half a dozen down in the alleyway and there could easily have

126

been another six already inside, maybe more. Maybe there were as many as twenty altogether, because it was a huge store. And when you think how long it takes you to clean the inside of one house, well Scottley's was as big as a hundred houses, maybe even a thousand.

The sound of the cleaning machines came from both above and beneath us and from all sides. We were surrounded. It was like this great army of ants was sweeping through the place, devouring everything in their path. And soon they'd find their way into the *Staff Only* section and then they'd find us.

And then we'd be for it.

'Mum,' I said, going into serious panic mode. 'What're we going to do? Where are we going to go? We've got to hide – and quick!'

'Oh, goody,' little Angeline said, as soon as she heard me say hide. 'Hide and seek. Baggsy I go first. You count to twenty.'

'I mean hide *for real*, Angeline,' I snapped. 'It's not a game.' But she didn't understand.

Only where could we hide? You can't really hide from cleaners, can you? At least not good ones, because good cleaners clean everywhere. We couldn't hide in the broom cupboard because they might open the door to get a broom out of it. We couldn't really hide in a toilet cubicle because they'd try all the doors so as to get in and pour green stuff into the toilet bowls.

Yet there had to be somewhere to hide in a store as big as Scottley's. Perhaps we could leg it up to the top of the emergency staircase and get out on to the roof, I thought. Or maybe we could go the other way, down into the lower basement where the heating boilers lived, and we could hide there. The cleaners surely wouldn't go dusting in the maintenance area. You didn't bother much with places like that. You just left them to the mice and the rats and the stowaways.

But Mum didn't seem like she was going to do anything. She simply stood there by the window with a dreamy, faraway look on her face, watching the cleaners get the last of the things out of their vans.

'There's always somebody busy, isn't there?' she said. 'Even on a Sunday morning. Life goes on, doesn't it? It's always going on somewhere.'

I grabbed her arm and shook it hard.

'Mum,' I said, 'we've got to *do* something. Got to hide somewhere. Got to do something and *quick*. Please!'

'It's all right, Livvy,' she said. 'Not to worry. Just carry on as if you've every right to be here and it'll be fine.'

'But Mum—'

But it was too late to say any more. A door had opened far down along the corridor and I could hear footsteps and the voices of two women approaching in our direction. It was too late to hide anywhere. We were as good as caught. Our secret would be out any second. Next the police would come and we'd all be arrested for spending the night in Scottley's.

'Come on, you two,' Mum said, cool as you please, 'let's get back to work.' And she went over to Henry and turned him on, and little Angeline followed her example and went back to spreading the dust around. So what could I do? I didn't know what to do. So I picked up my tin of polish and returned to work as well.

The voices got nearer. I could make out what they were saying now.

'Yeah, I said to him, it's all right for you to have a lie-in on a Sunday, but that doesn't mean that I can. I have to get up and got to Scottley's.'

'I know. It's not what you'd prefer, working on

a Sunday morning, but the money comes in handy and—'

They rounded the corner and stopped. There they were: two women armed to the teeth with dusters and mops and aerosols, one of them with a Henry of her own. They were both about my mum's age and looked as if they'd have children like us at home too. They stopped and stared at us, seeming slightly surprised for a moment, then the smaller of the two ladies called over to my mum.

'You all right, love? You doing *Staff Only* today as well?'

'Yes,' my mum said cheerfully, '*Staff Only* this morning.'

'Here, you're new, aren't you?' the larger of the two women asked.

'That's right,' Mum nodded. 'Only my second day here.'

'Thought I hadn't seen you before,' the larger woman went on. 'How're you finding it?'

'Not too bad,' Mum said.

'You're doing a good job here,' the smaller woman said, looking round admiringly at the cleaning we had done. 'But you don't need to be too fussy, not in *Staff Only*. It's the main store you have to worry about.'

'We're doing it for our cornflakes,' Angeline chimed in.

Oh no, I thought. *She's going to tell them. She's going to spill all the beans.*

But no. The smaller lady just patted little Angeline on the head and said, 'Doing it for cornflakes, are you? Well, well, now. That's nice, isn't it? Helping Mummy for cornflakes, are we? There's a good girl.'

The larger lady looked at Mum.

'You weren't in our van, were you? Whose van did you come in? Caroline's, was it? Or Len's? Or are you local?'

'Yes,' Mum said. 'Local.'

'Ah, got here under your own steam then?' the larger lady said.

'That's it,' Mum smiled. And she did a bit of energetic polishing, like she was anxious to get on with her work.

'Handy to live local,' the larger lady said. She seemed a bit nosey to me. 'You're quite close then?'

'Oh, yes,' Mum said, 'we almost live on top of the place.'

You can say that again, I thought. You couldn't get much more local or more on top of the place than the Bedding Department and that was a fact.

'Well, don't you take any nonsense, mind, that's my advice to you,' the larger lady said. 'Carter's isn't a bad firm to work for, but you've got to watch them sometimes or they'll get your hours wrong. A lot of people don't stay long, always coming and going and chopping and changing, aren't they, Marge?'

'Yes,' Marge agreed. 'New faces all the time. I never know half of them, they're changing that often.'

Mum looked a bit relieved at this.

'You should be all right with the kids though,' the lady who wasn't Marge said. 'They don't mind you bringing them with you, just as long as they don't touch nothing.'

'Oh, they wouldn't do that,' Mum said.

'We're helping, not touching,' little Angeline said, and she got another pat on the head for that.

'There's a good girl, helping Mummy,' Marge said. Then she turned to Mum, 'On your own, are you, with the kids?'

'Yes,' Mum nodded. 'Their father's abroad. He's . . . a builder.'

'I thought you said he was on an oil rig!' I said.

'Yes, he builds oil rigs, Livvy, now don't interrupt.'

'Wasn't what you said before.'

'That'll do.'

'Oh, it's difficult, isn't it,' Marge nodded sympathetically, 'bringing them up on your own, especially when you have to work as well. It's never easy.'

I felt a bit narked with her then for saying that, and with Mum too for standing there nodding in agreement. If Marge thought it was hard for Mum bringing us up on her own, what did she think it was like for *me*, bringing *Mum* up on *my* own? And having a little sister to bring up too. She didn't know the half of it. I'd have told her all about it if she'd stayed much longer and that really would have given the game away.

'Okay,' the lady who wasn't Marge said, 'we'll let you get on here then and we'll go and start down at the other end.'

'Right you are,' Mum said. 'See you again.'

'I should think so,' Marge said, and off the two ladies went with their cleaning materials and their own little Henry, off in the direction of the staff canteen.

Once they were out of sight and earshot, Mum started to chuckle and she gave us a great big grin.

'There,' she boasted. 'I said it would be all right.

133

You see, we're cleaners now. No need to worry at all, was there, Livvy?'

And she was so pleased with herself I felt really annoyed. It was just like somebody had run across a road and had narrowly avoided being squashed by a bus. And all they could do afterwards was jig about going 'Na, na, nee, na, na. Missed me that time!' and stand sticking out their tongue and making out they'd been really clever instead of dead reckless and stupid.

But Mum just seemed to have no sense of danger at all.

'See, now that they think we're cleaners, we can go anywhere in the store. And it won't matter if they see us every day. In fact, they'll probably *expect* to see us. So we're all right.'

'What do you mean Mum – see us *every day*?' I asked. 'I thought we were only staying here until tomorrow.'

'Yes,' Mum said, looking a bit caught-out. 'That's what I meant, we'll be all right even if they see us again tomorrow.'

But she just aroused my suspicions all over again.

'And another thing, Mum,' I said. 'What about when all the cleaners leave? Won't they think it funny that we're staying behind?'

'No need for them to know. We'll just – disappear for a while. Come on, let's finish paying for those cornflakes.'

So off we went and did a bit more cleaning. Then, when it seemed that we had paid for the cornflakes about ten times over, we took all the cleaning stuff and carried it up the back stairs to the top floor. And whenever we met another cleaner, Mum would nod hello and say, 'Just got a bit to do up top,' and they'd say, 'Right you are, dear,' or something and up we went.

Finally we got to the very top, to Customer Accounts and Credit, right next to School Uniforms and Children's Shoes. There was a big sofa there for customers to sit on while they waited to be attended to.

'Here,' Mum said, 'this'll do.'

And so we sat on the sofa and played I Spy until the sound of the cleaners beneath us got further and further away as they worked their way down through the store. Then finally all the vacuum cleaners and the floor polishers fell silent, and then there were voices out in the side alleyway again, and then the noise of doors slamming and of people shouting, 'All here then? Ready to go?' And then the vans drove away and all was quiet. And Scottley's was ours once more.

CHAPTER NINE

What to do next? It was maybe about eleven thirty and there was a good hour and a half to lunch.

What to do to fill the day? It was a long time till tomorrow. A long time until I had to go to school again and little Angeline had to attend the nursery. A long time until Monday, until Mum could call in at the Housing Office and find us somewhere proper to live. A long time until we could move out of Scottley's. I'd never known a day seem so unending. It lay before us like a railway track, stretching on and on to the horizon.

'Mum,' I said, 'can't we go out?'

It was a nice sunny day outside. I wanted to go to a park, or for a walk down by the river. The novelty of being in Scottley's had suddenly worn off. It didn't seem so great any more. I felt hemmed-in and trapped, and I wanted to see the sky – properly, not just through a window.

Little Angeline agreed with me.

'Go to a park,' she said. 'Go on the swings.'

Mum actually looked worried.

'I don't know if we can, Angel, I'm afraid that if we open any of the doors, it might set the burglar alarms off.'

'But we won't be breaking in,' Angeline said, 'we'll be breaking out.'

'Yes,' Mum said, 'but the alarms don't know that. They'll go off anyway.'

'Cleaners got in with the alarms going off,' Angeline pointed out.

'Yes,' Mum said, 'but they had keys and they must have known the alarm code.'

'So do you mean to say, Mum,' I said, getting on my high horse, 'that we cannot even go out and get some proper fresh air, like children ought to be able to if they're ever to grow up properly and stay healthy?'

I could tell I'd hurt her a bit saying that and I immediately wished I hadn't.

'It's only for a day, Livvy, just one day, that's all. Just imagine that it's pouring down with rain outside and that you don't want to go out anyway.'

'But the sun's shining.'

'Just imagine though.'

138

'Well, if we can't go out, what *can* we do?'

'Go exploring round the store. But you're not to damage anything.'

'Can we see if there's anything on TV?'

'All right, I suppose so. Come on then. Let's see what we can find.'

So first we took all the cleaning stuff back to where it belonged, then we went off in search of the Radio, Television and Stereo Department to see if there was anything good on the telly.

There must have been a hundred TV sets there at the very least, all sitting on top of each other like building blocks, as if the whole side wall of the department was made out of TVs.

They were all grey and blank.

'How do you put them on, Mum?'

'I'm not sure,' she said, looking about for a switch. She found a remote control handset behind one of the counters and she pressed the on button – but nothing happened.

'Must be off at the mains,' she said. 'Hold on.'

She went behind the counter again and I went with her and we found a whole load of switches.

'Try that one,' I suggested. So she did, and a ceiling light came on.

'No,' Mum said. 'Let's try another.'

This time a radio came on.

'Another.'

This time piped music came on over the intercom system.

'No, must be this one.'

And finally the television came on. Or rather, *all* the televisions came on, the whole hundred of them, all at once, all with the same picture.

'Whoopee!' little Angeline cried out. 'Look! TV wallpaper.'

'We can watch a set each!' I said.

'We can watch about thirty sets each,' Mum said. 'So what's on?' And she took the remote control and flicked though the channels.

There were loads of channels too. Scottley's must have been connected to all the cable and satellite stations and able to receive just about every channel in the world. There were foreign language stations and non-stop children's programmes with films and cartoons showing all day.

'I want this one!' Angeline said, when a Tom and Jerry cartoon came on. But I'd seen it before and I wanted another programme, and Mum wanted another one still.

The trouble was that all the sets seemed to get the same programme at the same time, and it took Mum about a quarter of an hour to work out how to get them on to different channels. But finally there they were. Thirty-odd sets tuned to the children's cartoons, thirty-odd sets tuned to the children's film I wanted to see, and the rest of the sets tuned to the chat show programme Mum wanted to watch.

But there was still the problem of the sound. You couldn't hear your own programme for the noise of the other two. But Mum borrowed some sets of earphones from the stereo demonstration equipment and she plugged them into the TVs – which had sockets for earphones – and then we sat and watched and listened to our own programmes without being bothered by either of the others.

And it was great really. There were no chairs for us; but it didn't matter, we just sprawled on the carpet. But Mum must have tiptoed away at some point and gone down to Soft Furnishings, because she suddenly appeared with three beanbags – so big you couldn't see her behind them and it looked as if walking beanbags were coming down the aisle to get you – and she dropped them to the floor and we lay on them.

It was great, really great, and we must have spent an hour or more there, just lying on our beanbags and watching the telly, and I forgot all about the sunny day outside for a while. Eventually though, Mum said that we'd seen enough telly for a while and it was time to tune them back to how they'd been before (all receiving the same channel) and to turn them off and to carry the bean bags down to Soft Furnishings and to maybe see about a spot of lunch.

So that was what we did. We went to the Food Hall and we found some cheese in the cold cabinet, just right on its expiry date, so it was all right to have it. So we took the cheese up to the canteen, got our bread out of the fridge and we made cheese sandwiches for lunch.

After lunch, when it must have been half past one or so, I began hankering to go outside again. Mum said that maybe we should try the Toy Department if we were getting bored, so we did. We found a demonstration frisbee there and had a game with it – though little Angeline wasn't really big enough to catch it on her own, so you had to catch it for her and pretend that she'd caught it herself, or give her very easy throws. And you know, that Toy Department was so big that not even Mum could throw the frisbee from one end of it to the other. In fact that Toy Department was so big it almost went into another time zone.

I kept on badgering Mum for us to go out. Scottley's had begun to feel like some great luxurious prison. And what use, I thought, are all the toys and tellies and frisbees and soft furnishings and beanbags and cheese sandwiches past their sell-by date in the world if you can't even go outside.

'Okay, Livvy,' Mum said at last, when I'd finally worn her down. 'Let's see what we can do. Maybe there *is* a way of going outside without setting off the burglar alarms. Come on you two, follow me and bring the frisbee.'

And with that she left the Toy Department and headed for the escalator. But instead of going down to the ground floor, she went *up*.

'Where we going?' little Angeline kept saying, as we marched on up through the departments. 'There's no outside up here. Only more inside. Outside isn't upstairs, outside is downstairs and out through the door.'

'Come on,' I said. 'It'll be all right. I think I know where we're going.'

And sure enough we were. We were heading for the roof.

We got to the last department and found the emergency stairs. We followed them up as far as they went, walked along a short corridor, and then found another set of stairs which had a sign on the wall by them pointing to the roof garden. And then we came to a door.

'Okay,' Mum said, 'now let's have a look.'

She studied the door carefully, looking at every inch of it, running her fingers around the rim, feeling for any wires that might have it connected to the burglar alarm.

'No,' she said. 'Seems okay. I don't suppose they're expecting anyone to break in from the roof. You couldn't really. You couldn't get up here from the outside. Not unless you were a burglar with his own helicopter . . . well, it's a risk . . . but if you really want to go out . . . here goes.'

And she pushed the bar and the door opened.

We stood there a moment, waiting for the alarm to go off. What if it *did* and we had to run for it? We hadn't even packed our suitcase.

But no. Silence. Only the familiar sound of the traffic coming from far, far below. Not very loudly either, as it was Sunday and the city was quiet.

Mum said. 'Seems all right. Just let me jam the door open so that we can get back in.' And while I held the door, she got an old plastic chair which someone had left out up there and she used it to wedge the door open. Then we all trooped out on to the roof.

There was a nice little garden there too and there were chairs and sun loungers, as if the staff at Scottley's went up on to the roof in the summer to sunbathe during their lunch hours.

The wall around the roof was quite high, so there was no chance of anybody accidentally falling off. But there were little gaps in it here and there, just like the slits in a castle wall, so that you could peek out and admire the view and see the street far below. It gave you butterflies in your stomach to think what a long way down to the ground it was. It seemed like miles.

The roof itself was enormous, at least the size of a football pitch, and part of it was covered in artificial grass. You could have ridden a bike around it and I asked Mum if we could bring some bikes up from Children's Bicycles, Skateboards and Roller Blades, but she didn't think it was such a good idea. She said it was too far to carry them

145

and anyway the bikes might get damaged or scratched.

So we played with the frisbee again instead, being careful not to throw it over the wall, and when we got tired of that we played Hide and Seek. Not that there were many places to hide on the roof; but there were a few, like behind the air duct outlets and the huge air-conditioning unit and things like that. And when we got fed up with Hide and Seek, we just lay down on the artificial grass and sprawled out under the weak, pale sunshine, and we shielded our eyes and counted the aeroplanes as they flew overhead, and we watched their jet trails get longer and longer, just like Pinocchio's nose.

We waved at the pilots and the stewards and stewardesses and all the passengers on board. I wondered if they could see us and whether they waved back, but they were probably too far away. But maybe they *could* see us. And what a story it would make when they landed, about the children they had seen as they flew over some strange, unfamiliar city; the children they had seen on the great, high roof, waving their hands at them; the highest-up children in the world. And that's who we were and I said so to Angeline.

'We're the highest-up children in the world, Angeline.'

'Yes,' she said. 'We are. And Mum's the highest-up mum in the world.'

And I supposed that was true too.

We must have been there a good long time and we didn't move until the breeze blew up a little and a slight chill came into the air as a cloud loomed overhead. And I looked at Mum and saw that she was just lying there, looking at the sky. And she seemed as far away as one of those aeroplanes. I thought she must be thinking of Dad and how she wished he could be with us, lying there, on Scottley's roof.

And I felt almost happy for a while. Happy and a bit sad. I liked it there, up on Scottley's roof. It was nice to be the highest-up in the world, even if you knew it couldn't last. It was so peaceful, so nice. You'd have liked it, you really would.

CHAPTER TEN

But then it got quite cold and we had to come in, and I began to worry all over again.

'Mum,' I asked, as we walked back down the escalators towards the Food Hall, 'where are we going to sleep tonight? I mean, what about the security patrol? What if he comes back into the Bedding Department while we're all asleep and this time he hears little Angeline gurgling and you snoring.'

'I don't snore!' Mum said. 'Don't be cheeky.'

'And I don't gurgle,' little Angeline said, 'and don't be rude.' And she was so annoyed with me she gurgled with irritation.

I practically gave up on the both of them then. I was in half a mind to just turn my back on them and walk out of Scottley's forever and leave them to manage on their own. But I knew they'd never be able to, so I stayed.

'But Mum,' I said, 'we have to do *something*.'

'Don't worry,' she said, 'we'll work it out.'

She led the way into the Food Hall and we searched the freezers and the cold cabinets for something a bit past its sell-by date. It took us ages to find anything and the only thing we did find was a Leek and Potato Bake. Angeline said eeech!, she hated leeks, even if she never had tasted them, but she knew she didn't like them just from the picture on the front and the name.

'You couldn't like eating anything called leeks,' she said. 'No more than you could enjoy eating anything called drains. Or sinks. Or gutters. Because that's where leeks come from. In fact, I heard Mum say once that her hot-water bottle had sprung a leek. Well, I'm definitely not eating them if they grow in hot-water bottles and places like that. They'll taste all rubbery.'

Mum and I tried to explain to her that this was a different kind of leek, that there was a leek and a leak and you ate one but not the other and they were spelt differently anyway. But Angeline couldn't be persuaded.

I didn't fancy the Leek and Potato Bake much myself, but there was no choice, so we took it off to the staff canteen along with an apple pie we had found which also needed eating and we warmed the two things up and had them for our tea.

The Leek and Potato Bake wasn't so bad after all, at least not when you smothered it in ketchup. And the apple pie was delicious and didn't need any ketchup at all.

We washed everything up then and as it was too early to go to bed yet, I asked Mum if we could go back to play in the Toy Department; but she said no, we'd done enough of that for a day. So Angeline asked if we could go and watch thirty televisions each again in the TV and Electrical. But Mum said we'd seen enough TV and Electrical for the day too.

When I asked her what we *could* do then, she said we could go to the Books Department and read for a while. But we weren't to get any books dirty or to fold any page corners back to mark our places or anything like that.

So off we went to the Books Department and there were loads of books there for all ages – even for Angeline, who's not much good at reading though she's hot stuff when it comes to looking at the pictures. She's very advanced at looking at pictures and I reckon that if there was an exam for looking at pictures, she'd come in top. Because she doesn't just look at little pictures, she looks at big ones too.

Now, before we got to the Books Department, we first made a little diversion. We went down to Domestic Appliances with all our dirty washing in a Scottley's carrier bag, in the hope that there might be a washing machine there (maybe a demonstration model) which was all plumbed in and ready to go.

Well, we looked at them all, but none of them seemed to be connected to a water tap, so we were out of luck. But then I had a brain-wave. They were bound to need a washing machine that worked in a big place like Scottley's. Because what about all the staff uniforms and all the tablecloths for the restaurants and all the towels in the shower room and the rest? Maybe most of it was sent to outside cleaners, but there had to be at least one washing machine in the place, if only for emergencies, like when a waiter spilt some dinner over a customer's best trousers.

So I mentioned this to Mum and she agreed, and we had a good look round all the *Staff Only* corridors until we found a door marked *Service*, and we pushed it open, and there it was, a washing machine all connected up. And next to it was a tumble drier too, and next to that was an ironing board and an iron, all ready to be used.

So in went the washing and off we went to the Books Department.

Once we'd chosen some books and had lain down on the carpet to read them, Mum said she'd be back in fifteen minutes and we weren't to go away. When I asked where she was going, she said, 'exploring various possibilities.' Angeline said she wanted to go exploring possibilities too as she'd never explored a possibility before and was it like a cave? But Mum insisted that we had to stay there together in the Books Department and off she went.

She was gone longer than fifteen minutes; it was more like half an hour and I was starting to get a bit worried. (You know me.) But she finally returned and she had our big suitcase with her, all packed and ready to go (apart from the clothes that were in the washing machine, of course).

'Okay,' Mum said, 'come on girls, we're moving.'

My heart leapt. *Moving!* I could have kissed her from sheer relief. We were getting out of Scottley's. No more non-stop worrying about being caught and getting into trouble. We were off to a new home. Mum had found us somewhere new. I didn't know how she'd done it, but as long as she had, that was all that mattered.

'Where're we going Mum? Where to? How did you find somewhere so quickly? You haven't been out, have you?'

And then my hopes were dashed.

'Oh, no, we're not moving out of Scottley's. We're staying here in the store. We're just moving out of Beds and Bedding and going to a different department.'

My heart sank.

'Where, Mum? Exactly *where* are we going now?'

'Well,' she said, with a bit of mischief in her voice, 'I thought we could all go camping.'

'Whoopeee!' little Angeline yelled, 'I love camping!'

'Camping?' I said. 'In Scottley's? How on earth can you go camping in a *shop*? Camping is outside. Not inside. How can we possibly go *camping*, Mum!' And I felt that she'd finally gone and lost all her marbles, and that I'd need to ring for a white van to come and take her away to a rest home.

'Follow me,' Mum said, 'and you'll see.'

'Can we come back and finish our books after?' Angeline asked.

'If there's time. Ready?'

'Okay.'

So off we went. By then I'd already worked out where we were heading. We were going to the Sports, Outdoors and Camping Department, that part of the shop where they sold things like sleeping bags and rucksacks and little gas stoves – and tents.

Sports, Outdoors and Camping was down in the basement, just across the way from Gardening, Garden Furniture and Tools. There were tents everywhere, all put up on display – at least a dozen of them – ranging from one-man tents to tents the size of bungalows.

'It's not quite as convenient as the Bedding Department,' Mum said, just like she was discussing the merits of a new house we were moving to, 'but Sports, Outdoors and Camping does have its advantages, as you'll see.'

'Tents,' Angeline said. 'Camping. We're going on our hodilays.'

'Holidays!' I corrected her.

'Yes,' she said, still getting it wrong, 'hodilays, that's what I said.'

I felt I could have given her a good shake. Her

fitting in so readily with Mum's plans just seemed to encourage Mum and to make her worse than ever.

Mum smiled. 'That's it, Angeline, yes, we're going on our holidays. We're having a camping holiday. That's right.'

And Angeline went off to explore inside the tents.

'Mum . . . Mum—,' I began, about to start on another of my lectures.

'Now, I'll tell you what the advantages are,' she bulldozed on, completely ignoring me. 'First the tents are quite a way from the aisles. Now, I don't think the security man bothers to leave the aisle. He just patrols along it. So he won't come near to us. Secondly, we'll be inside a tent, so he's not going to see us. And thirdly, even if Angeline does gurgle while she's asleep—'

'I do not!' her voice called from inside an igloo-shaped tent. 'I have never gurgled in my life! I've only ever seen pictures of gurgles. I've never actually done any!'

'We're not saying you do,' Mum called back. 'It's just in case you *might*.'

'Well, I don't!' Then, 'Hey, it's great inside here,' she said. 'There's a little table.' And she forgot all about gurgles and gurgling for a while, until she started singing, 'What are gurgles made of? What are little gurgles made of? Rum and gum and wind in your tum. That's what gurgles are made of.'

Mum turned back to me, leaving Angeline to mess about inside the tent.

'As I was saying, Livvy, thirdly, even if someone does make a noise, like a gurgle or a snore . . .'

'Or an *Ahhhhhh!*?' I suggested, all innocence, but Mum ignored that too.

'. . . the security patrolman probably won't even notice.'

'Why not?'

'Listen,' Mum said. 'And you'll know.'

So I stood and listened and there it was. Why I hadn't already noticed it was a mystery. It was the gurgle of a fountain and the murmuring of a waterfall, coming from just across the way in Gardening, Garden Furniture and Tools. I went over to see it and there it was, nestling in amongst the wheelbarrows and the garden forks and the garden gnomes and the special gadgets for trimming the edges of your lawn. It was a complete ornamental fountain and waterfall and it made a lovely sound – not the sort of sound to keep you awake, more one that would help you sleep.

'We can imagine that we're out in the country,' Mum said, 'as we lie in our tent. It'll be nice, won't it?'

Well, I didn't agree about it being nice, because I wasn't in the mood for that; but I had to admit that Mum had a point. The security man was unlikely to hear anyone gurgling or snoring above the tinkling of that fountain and the splashing of that waterfall. He'd probably walk right past us without a thought.

'Okay,' I said, 'but I want a tent as far away from the aisle as possible, one right up by the wall.'

'All right,' Mum said, 'let's find one.'

So we went and coaxed little Angeline out of the igloo tent – which she didn't want to leave – and we found a nice big family-sized tent over by the wall. It was very well equipped inside, with folding beds which were quite comfy really, and there were sleeping bags on top of them and everything you needed – even a little battery-powered lantern hanging from the tent post.

'Well, Livvy?' Mum said.

'Okay,' I grudgingly agreed, 'it'll do. But just

one night. And tomorrow we go? Promise?'

'I know, Livvy,' she said, 'I know. Now I must go and sort out the washing. You two can go back up and finish reading your books if you want to, then it'll be time for bed.'

But it was all very well her saying, 'I know, Livvy, I know,' but she still hadn't exactly *promised* about the one night only, had she? I hadn't heard her make a promise or seen her cross her heart and hope to die.

Anyway, Angeline and I lay on the beds in the tent for a while, enjoying being under canvas and having the roof so near to us that we could reach up and touch it. Then we went back up to the Books Department to finish reading and looking at pictures.

Mum found us there about an hour later. She had done all the washing and our clothes were dried, ironed and neatly folded.

'Okay,' she said, 'bedtime.'

We put all the books back up on their shelves, just as we had found them. I said I thought that Angeline's doll ought to be returned to the Toy Department too, as we probably wouldn't have time to take it up there in the morning, and for once Mum agreed with me. I expected Angeline to make a fuss about parting with the doll but she was really good.

'I know it's the shop's and not mine,' she said. 'I'm not a baby, you know. I do understand.'

So we carried it up to the Toy Department and put it back where it belonged. Angeline said goodnight to it and told it not to leave its eyes open all night and to try and keep its knickers dry. Then we went down to *Staff Only*, had more showers, washed our hair and brushed our teeth, and then we were ready for bed.

Angeline and I got into our sleeping bags. Mum said that she would sit outside the tent for a little while and enjoy the sunset and see if she couldn't spot any zebras. (I think she was trying to be funny. She does try to make jokes sometimes, I'm afraid.) So we all said goodnight.

I lay there until Angeline had fallen asleep, then I got up and went out of the tent to join Mum who was sitting at a table, staring into nothingness, just listening to the tinkling of the fountain and the waterfall and thinking her thoughts.

'Mum—'

'Livvy! You gave me a start. I thought you were asleep.'

'Mum, we *have* got an alarm clock to wake us up

in good time tomorrow, have we?'

'Yes, don't worry—'

'Because if we oversleep, Mum, and wake up at nine o'clock and Scottley's is full of customers and assistants, and there we are, all lying in our sleeping bags in one of their tents, all in our pyjamas—'

'Don't worry, Livvy, don't worry—'

'But what if the alarm clock doesn't go off?'

'I'll borrow an extra one from the Clocks Department.'

'Borrow two, Mum.'

'All right, two then.'

'Mum . . .'

'Yes, Livvy?'

'How are we going to get out in the morning without anyone seeing us?'

'Livvy, you worry too much.'

'Yes, I know. But how are we?'

'It'll be all right. We'll just need to get up a bit early.'

'But—'

'Don't worry. Go to bed now, okay? Don't worry. It'll be fine.'

Well, I didn't think it would be fine, but I kissed her and went to bed anyway, and I must have been quite tired as I fell asleep almost immediately and I didn't wake until seven in the morning, when I heard three alarm clocks all going off together – our own clock and the two that Mum had borrowed from Clocks, Watches and Timepieces. And quite a dawn chorus *that* was.

And if the security patrolman had come along through the Sports, Outdoors and Camping Department in the small hours of the night – well, I hadn't heard him. And I don't suppose he could have heard us either, or he'd have woken us up and told us so and then probably have arrested us or something.

But we hadn't been arrested. We were still at large. Yes, somehow Mum had got away with it again. But how much longer would our luck hold out?

CHAPTER ELEVEN

Drrrring! Drrrring!

Meep-meep-meep!

Nee-naw, nee-naw, nee-naw!

The three alarm clocks all went on making a terrible racket until Mum thumped them off.

'Okay, girls,' she said, getting out of her sleeping bag and going straight into action. 'Let's get going. No time to lose. Here, get dressed and give me your pyjamas.'

In minutes we were dressed, our hair was combed and Mum was packing our pyjamas up in the big suitcase.

'Right, breakfast,' she said.

So off we went to the Food Hall, found some more just-out-of-date milk and took it up to the staff canteen. We got what was left of our bread out of the fridge, toasted it in the big toaster and finished off the cereal while we were at it. We ate breakfast quickly, washed everything up, and then hurried back down to Sports, Outdoors and Camping for our coats and to get my school things.

When I was ready, Mum locked the big suitcase and looked around for somewhere to hide it.

'But Mum,' I objected. 'I thought you said it was just for two nights, that we weren't coming back here, that—'

'Yes, Livvy,' she snapped, 'I know. But I don't want to lug this big heavy suitcase about with me all day, not all round to the Housing Office and everywhere. We'll leave it here for now and pick it up this afternoon or this evening, before they close.'

'But Mum . . .' and my poor old heart was sinking again. The number of times it's sunk too! One day it's going to go right down to the bottom of the ocean and never come up again. It's not easy when you've got a sinking heart. Some people's hearts – like Mum's – they always seem to be bobbing about on the crest of the wave. But my heart's the sinking kind; it never learned how to swim. I reckon it should have its own life-jacket to keep it afloat and its own emergency flares for when it needs to be rescued.

Mum hid the big suitcase inside one of the tents.

She left it under a camp bed where no one could see it. It was a bit of a risk just the same, because somebody might have gone in to try the tent out and have sat down on the bed and then they'd have found it there. But then, as Mum's always saying, all life's a risk really and nothing's ever that certain – though I wish it was.

I noticed that Mum kept glancing at her watch and as eight o'clock drew nearer, even she began to seem nervous.

'Come on then, girls,' she said. 'They'll all be arriving soon. I think we ought to make ourselves scarce.'

You see, the problem was that all of the staff arrived at about eight o'clock, but the doors weren't opened to the customers until half-past. The staff spent that intervening half-hour getting things ready. If the doors had been opened to the public at eight, it would have been okay. We could have pretended that we were early shoppers browsing round the store, and then we could have nipped out at the first opportunity. But as it was, we had to hide up for at least half an hour.

Only *where*?

And another thing. If we hid up for much more than half an hour, what about me? I'd never get to school in time. I had to be there by five to nine at the very latest and the school was a good twenty minutes away from Scottley's, even on the bus. In fact it was usually quicker to walk, as the traffic was so bad. So what about that? What about me?

'Where, Mum? Where are we going to hide?' I asked, and I looked up at the clock on the wall and the second hand was zooming round.

'Just a minute,' she said. 'Let me think . . . There's the roof I suppose . . .'

But that seemed dangerous to me. You could only get to the roof by going up the *Staff Only* stairs. What if someone saw us in the *Staff Only* area? What excuse could we give for being there?

'I know,' she said. 'The ladies'! Customer ladies' that is, not staff ladies'. That'll be safe. We'll go there.'

So the ladies' it was.

Now the ladies' might have been dangerous too, even the customer ladies'. It was possible that some staff member might go into the customer ladies before the store opened, just to check it was all fresh and smelling nice; but we weren't at any risk from the cleaners themselves.

We had found a copy of the cleaning rota,

pinned to the wall of the staff canteen notice board. Cleaning took place every evening after the store closed – except on a Saturday. There was no cleaning on Saturday evening, but the shop was given a good top-to-bottom dusting on the Sunday morning, as we'd seen. So for now we were safe from the cleaners. Monday morning was a cleaner-free-zone.

So in we went to the customer ladies' and we all squeezed into one cubicle, locked the door, and waited.

And tried not to laugh.

Well, I tell you, that was one of the hardest things I've ever done. We were half an hour in that cubicle in the ladies', the three of us, all squashed in there like we were a load of sardines. It was so hard not to giggle, it really was. And it was rather uncomfortable too, standing there all cramped together; so we took it in turns to sit on the seat – well, the lid anyway. We had five minutes each; though to be honest, little Angeline got to sit down all the time, because even when it wasn't her turn I let her perch on my knee and Mum allowed her too as well. So she did all right, really.

Outside, beyond the door of the ladies', we could hear the muffled Monday morning sounds of the great department store coming alive. There were bangs and thuds, voices and shouts, faint calls of 'Good morning' and 'Did you have a nice weekend?'

But then we heard a sound which struck terror into us – even into Mum, who's pretty fearless most of the time. It was the click-clack-click of stiletto heels approaching along the corridor, and they stopped right outside the customer ladies' – no more than a few yards away from us.

'Quick,' Mum hissed. 'Up on the seat or they might see our feet!'

So the three of us got up and perched on the seat in the cubicle.

'And not a sound!' Mum cautioned. 'Not a whisper.'

'But Mum,' little Angeline hissed, 'but Mum, I need a wee.'

I nearly fell off the seat. I mean, it wasn't funny really, and yet it was. There we were, hiding in a cubicle in the ladies, all perched on top of the seat, all about to get into the most awful terrible trouble if we were caught, and Angeline had to say that.

'Just hold on,' Mum said. 'It's only for a moment.'

'But I can't!'

'Shhhh!'

The door opened. Two sets of stiletto heels clicked in, brisk, efficient and business-like.

'Customer ladies', Miss Greystone!' one voice said.

'Customer ladies', Mrs Gregg!' the second voice agreed.

'Up to standard and Scottley-shape, Miss Greystone?' the first voice spoke again.

'Clean and up to scratch, Mrs Gregg,' said the second.

'Kindly mark it in the book, Miss Greystone.'

'Kindly confirm that I have marked it in the book, Mrs Gregg.'

'Pleasure, Miss Greystone.'

'Thank you, Mrs Gregg.'

'On with the inspection, Miss Greystone.'

'Lead the way, Mrs Gregg!'

And the door swung to behind the departing voices and the clicking heels, and we were safe again for a while longer.

'I don't need a wee any more now,' Angeline told us.

'That,' Mum said, 'comes as no surprise to anyone.'

I looked at Mum's watch. It was eight twenty-seven.

'Mum,' I said, 'we ought to get going or I won't make it to school.'

'Okay,' she said, 'come on.'

We went to the door of the customer ladies' and waited; Mum stood watching the second hand of her watch go round. A few moments after eight-thirty a bell rang loudly throughout the store to indicate that it was time to throw the doors open and to let the customers in (or, as in our case, out).

'Okay,' Mum said, 'let's go.'

And out we went to the corridor.

There were several customer ladies' on various floors of the shop, but the one we were in was on the ground floor, just off from Handbags. Out we went and bustled brazenly through the aisles. One or two assistants did stare at us, wondering how we could have got into the shop so quickly when they had only just rung the bell to open the doors. But Mum just wished them a cheery good morning and asked the way to Children's Clothes and when they told her she said, 'Thanks very much,' and we hurried on.

Then we were out of the Handbags Department

and moving into Scottley's grand entrance hall.

But that was a mistake. We should have made for one of the side entrances. Because there he was, Mr Whiskers himself, standing right there at the front door.

And he gave us such a filthy look. Such a look! So full of suspicion that you'd have thought we were major criminals who were there to do a robbery and to pinch all the jewels from Scottley's famous Jewellery Department.

'Oi!' he said. 'How did you lot get in here? I never saw you come in.'

But Mum wasn't having any of it.

'Kindly open the door for us please, my man,' she said, all hoity-toity and putting him in his place. 'We won't need a cab today. The weather seems fine and I think we'll walk. No need to go to any trouble.'

And you know, he actually opened the door.

Well, to tell the truth, he didn't open it so that we could get out, but so that a rather grand lady who had just appeared outside could get in. But she was so nice and well-mannered she just said, 'After you, dear,' to Mum, and added, 'I know what it's like with children in tow. Please, you go ahead.'

'Thank you very much,' Mum said, and out we went, and poor old Mr Whiskers just had to stand there, going pink, then red, then purple; seething away to himself; holding the door open for us, just as if we were posh. And if you'd put a match to his whiskers right then, he'd have gone off like a rocket.

But it didn't matter, because we were out. At last we were out of Scottley's – out and free! We'd never have to go back there again, except to pick up our suitcase. By the evening we'd have a new place to stay, a new home that we could live in forever. Our moving days were over and Scottley's could be forgotten. It had been a great adventure, but it was over now and I was glad.

The only trouble was, as I discovered later on that day, it wasn't over at all. And I don't know why I'd ever thought it would be, not that easily. I should have known better really – and maybe a part of me did. In my heart of many hearts I think I knew that Mum had been too optimistic again. Her and her rose-coloured glasses.

I often wish she'd get another pair sometimes; a pair that didn't show things so pink and rosy, but more as they really are.

CHAPTER TWELVE

When we got to the school gates I realised that I didn't have any lunch. But Mum had remembered, and she took my lunch box out from her shoulder bag and handed it to me.

'What's in it?' I asked.

'Something nice,' she said. 'Must fly now. We want to get to the nursery in time, don't we, Angel? And then Mummy can be first to the Housing Office and see about our new house. We'll meet you here when school's over, Livvy. Okay?'

'Okay, I suppose,' I said. I didn't have much choice. So I kissed them both goodbye and watched them walk off down the road together. I opened my lunch box to see what was inside. There was an apple, a crunchy bar, a carton of orange juice and a Scottley's pre-packed cheese sandwich, slightly past its sell-by date. I had a feeling then that I was going to spend the rest of my life eating food that was slightly past its sell-by date. Not that the sandwich had gone stale or anything; it wasn't mouldy, or anything like that. It was just sort of second best; not what you'd choose to have if you could avoid it.

I went into school then. I said hello to a couple of people, but I didn't really have any close friends. It was because we were always moving. I'd be at a school just long enough to start making some really good friends and then we'd be off again. So I'd stopped trying. I was tired of making friends just to lose them all in a couple of months. But when I tried to explain this to Mum, she just said things like, 'Where's your sense of adventure, Livvy?' and 'You don't want to get stuck in a rut at your age, do you?'

But I did, really. I'd have been quite happy to be stuck in a rut for a few years, and the deeper and ruttier the better. But Mum would only go on about her itchy feet then and that gypsy in her soul. I got so fed up with her itchy feet, I just wished she'd give them a good long hard scratch and be done with it.

The rest of the day passed me by as if it was all somehow blurred and out of focus. I kept thinking about our adventure and how mad it had all been.

I looked at the teachers and at the headmaster and all the other children around me. *What would they say*, I wondered, *if they knew that we'd been living in Scottley's department store for the whole weekend? They'd be amazed, that's what. Astonished. Surprised. A bit jealous even, in some cases.*

I suddenly felt rather proud then and a bit chuffed, because I knew there were children in my class who came from big houses with two cars in the double garage and another one parked out on the drive, and they never had to eat sandwiches a bit past their sell-by date, and they'd been to Disney World and all over the place – but they hadn't lived for a whole weekend in Scottley's department store.

No, they hadn't slept in the Bedding Department. They hadn't lived in a tent down in Sports, Outdoors and Camping. They hadn't had a whole Toy Department all to themselves to play in, with big dolls that went Boo Hoo and which wet their knickers when you filled them up with water and which slept with their eyes open. They hadn't played frisbee up on the roof garden, with the aeroplanes above and the whole city beneath them. They hadn't eaten Fish Pie With Broccoli (slightly past its sell-by date) warmed up by a microwave in Kitchenware and Domestic Appliances. They hadn't had toast and cornflakes in the staff canteen or a shower in the staff showers or hidden three to a cubicle in customer ladies'. So they'd missed out on more than I had. Yes, it had been a wonderful two days – if somewhat nerve-wracking – but I was glad it was over.

I spent the rest of that day wondering what our new house would be like and where it would be. I imagined the fun we would have getting it sorted out. Maybe we'd have to do a bit of decorating, painting and wallpapering and stuff like that. Maybe Mum could write to Dad and tell him about the new house and he'd want so much to see it that he'd come home from the oil rigs. It would be funny to see him. I didn't remember him at all. He'd left to go and work on the oil rigs when Mum was expecting little Angeline and when I was still small. I knew I ought to remember him, I should have had some recollection, but I didn't. Not one. He didn't even seem real to me in some ways.

Three-fifteen came and school was over. I hung around in the playground, waiting for Mum and for Angeline to come and find me. They still weren't there at half past, but I wasn't worried.

Mum was never that great at time-keeping and there were still plenty of other children in the yard. But by twenty to four I was beginning to grow concerned, so I went to the gate and looked up and down the street. And finally I saw them coming, Mum bustling along and little Angeline having to trot to keep up with her.

'Livvy!' she called. 'Here! Sorry we're a bit late.'

'It's all right, Mum,' I said, 'You're only about half an hour late, that's all.' But you're wasting your time trying to be sarcastic with Mum, it's all water off a duck's back to her.

'Oh good,' she said. 'That's not so bad then. Right. Did you have a good day?'

'So-so,' I said. 'What about you? What happened at the Housing Office? Where's the new house? Have you seen it yet? Is it big or little? Is it far from the school? Will we have a bedroom each? I don't mind if we don't. I'm quite happy to share with Angeline. Does it need decorating? Do we have to paint it, shall we—'

But she stopped me in mid-flight.

'Livvy,' she said. 'There's been a bit of a problem.'

And my heart sank again, just like it's always sinking whenever Mum's plans go into action – and usually go wrong.

'Problem, Mum? What sort of problem?'

'Not a serious problem,' she said. 'Not one we have to worry about especially. It's just they still haven't got quite the place we wanted.'

'Mum,' I said, 'what do you mean?'

'I mean they've only got a flat free in Southfield at the moment.'

'So let's go there, Mum, that'll do, that'll be fine, that's okay.'

'It is not!' Mum said indignantly. 'There's no way we're going to live in a place like Southfield. It's the roughest neighbourhood in town. The things that go on there! Southfield is where all the stolen cars end up. And that's the least of it. Oh no. Certainly not. We've waited this long, we can wait a bit longer until what we want becomes available. No, you've got to make a stand, Livvy. You can't let them fob you off with any old thing. No, I'd rather live in Scottley's forever than accept a place on that Southfield estate.'

My heart sank to rock bottom and then started sinking through the rock as well.

'Yes, they tell everyone it's Southfield or nothing to start with,' Mum continued, 'but once you make it clear that you're not having it, they soon find you somewhere else ... Well, soonish.'

'So they *have* got somewhere else?' I said, and I almost cheered.

'Indeed they have,' Mum said, with a big grin on her face. 'They've got a nice little house out in Western View, and they say that we're something of a priority and that we'd be ideal tenants and we can have it.'

I did a little dance on the spot.

'We can have it? *Really* have it? Really, Mum, *really*? Our own house? We won't have to move any more? I can stay at the same school and make some friends and put down roots? Do you really mean it?'

'Course I do – don't I, Angeline?'

'Yes, Mum,' she said. (But then she'll say, 'Yes Mum,' to just about anything.)

'But what about the itchy feet, Mum?' I asked. 'And the gypsy in your soul? What'll you say to him?'

'I'll say to him: "Later. Later when the girls are grown up. Then we'll go wandering again." '

'Oh Mum, Mum, that's great. So there's not really a problem after all?'

'Nothing we can't overcome.'

'So when do we move in, Mum? Can we go there now? Have you got the keys?'

'Not on me, not at the moment. We can't move in immediately, there's just a bit of a wait while the people in there move out to their new house and while the council does some work on it.'

'So when will it be ready, Mum? After tea?'

'Em . . . not quite that soon. More . . . in about . . . a month.'

'*A month*?'

'Yes, A month. That's only four weeks though, Livvy. A month'll soon go by.'

'And where do we live in the meantime, Mum? Where do we stay until the house is ready? Where do we go?'

But I already knew the answer. I knew it before Mum even opened her mouth to speak.

'Well, it seems to me,' she said, 'that we might as well stay where we are for now.'

'But Mum, we aren't *anywhere*,' I protested, in one last ditch attempt to stave off the inevitable.

'Yes we are,' she said. 'We're living in Scottley's. It's done us for the weekend, I'm sure it can do us for a bit longer.'

My spirits sank down through the soles of my shoes and into the hard surface of the playground.

'Scottley's? Oh no, Mum! Not for four weeks. My nerves won't be able to stand it. I can't! Isn't there somewhere else? There must be.'

'Not as nice as Scottley's,' Mum said. 'Or as warm, or as convenient.'

'Scottley's,' little Angeline chimed in. 'Nice in Scottley's. Want to live in Scottley's for lots.'

I could have brained her. And Mum. I could have brained myself come to that. What a family! How did I ever get involved with them? It was beyond me. I'd half a mind to stop the next person who came down the street and to plead with them to adopt me. But no, I couldn't abandon Mum and Angeline. I knew they'd never survive without me. I just had to stick with them and do what I could to stop them from getting into too much trouble.

'Well, come on then,' said Mum. 'We'd best be getting home.'

'Scottley's,' little Angeline said. 'Scottley's is home.'

So off we went down the road. Home. To Scottley's.

Our luck got no better there.

As we drew near to the department store, Mum said, 'Let's not use the main entrance; that doorman with the whiskers will be there. Let's go to the side.'

So we went to the side entrance and who should we see there? That's right, Mr Whiskers himself. Maybe he'd got fed up with being on the main door and had swapped round with one of the other doormen for a while. But there he was, his big hairy whiskers sticking out everywhere, and as soon as he saw us they began to bristle.

'Ah ha!' he said. 'Now look—'

But Mum just breezed right past him.

'Lovely afternoon, isn't it?' she said. And before he could agree that it was or say that it wasn't, we were in through the door and heading for the escalator. I turned and saw him looking after us, and it was almost as if he *knew* – as if he *knew* that we'd moved into Scottley's, only he couldn't quite prove anything. But we'd better watch it, his whiskers seemed to say, because he'd catch us out sooner or later. And when he did, woe betide us . . .

'Where we going?' Angeline asked, once we were safely inside

'Let's have a cup of tea,' Mum said, 'I think we can afford that,' and she took us to the self-service cafeteria on the third floor.

I looked at the wall clock. It was twenty to five. The shop closed at five-thirty on Monday,

Tuesday and Wednesday, and at six o'clock on Thursday and Saturday. Our big problem was going to be on Friday when there was late-night shopping and the store remained open until eight.

Mum got herself a tea and bought us some juice and we sat at a table, killing time.

'I'm hungry,' little Angeline said. 'Got any sell-bys, Mum?'

She'd started calling things to eat 'sell-bys' and now used the expression for all sorts of food.

'Got any sell-by biscuits, Mum?' she'd say. 'Got any sell-by chocolate? Got any sell-by sell-bys?'

I could tell what little Angeline was going to grow up into. I could see her when she was an old, old lady having the vicar round to tea, offering him a cup of tea and a plate of sell-bys.

'We'll get some sell-bys later,' Mum said. 'When everyone's gone.'

'Mum,' I said, feeling a bit anxious again.

'What now, Livvy?'

'How're we going to stay in here when they lock up? We can't hide under the beds in the Bedding Department again, can we? Where can we hide this time when they close the store?'

'Don't worry,' Mum said. 'We'll find somewhere.'

'Well, we'll have to find it pretty soon,' I pointed out.

'No need to panic, Livvy,' Mum said. 'That won't do any good.'

But I couldn't help but worry about us getting caught. It was a terrible strain on me, all this living in Scottley's. I didn't know how much more of it I could take.

I caught a glimpse of my reflection in one of the cafeteria windows. I was sure I was getting wrinkles. It was probably all the worry.

Then little Angeline piped up.

'Mum,' she said, 'can we play Hide in the Cubicle again? Like we played this morning? I liked that. That was a good game. This time I can pretend to be a toilet brush. And you can pretend to be a roll of loo paper. And Livvy can pretend to be a bar of soap.'

'What a good idea, Angel,' Mum said, 'you are a clever girl. Yes, let's all do that, shall we?'

'But I don't want to be a bar of soap!' I protested. But Mum carried on as if she hadn't heard me.

'Yes, we'll finish our drinks and then go and have a look in the Toy Department and then, when it's almost half past five, we'll go and play Hide in the Cubicle.'

And so that was what we did. We hid in the cubicle in customer ladies' again, pretending to be loo rolls and bars of soap, until it sounded as though everyone had gone, then out we came and down we went to Sports, Outdoors and Camping Equipment to find our big suitcase.

Sure enough, there it was, under the camp bed where Mum had hidden it.

'Okay,' Mum said, 'we'll leave it for now. Just as long as we know that it's all right. Now, let's go and get something to eat for tea.'

So up we went to the Food Hall and we looked through all the cold cabinets and displays until we found some sell-bys. Then we took the sell-bys to the staff canteen, warmed them up and ate them. It was sell-by fish and chip suppers this time and very nice they were too. We had some peas with it as well. The peas weren't sell-bys but Mum said that we could pay for them by doing some more cleaning later. So after tea we went and got Henry the vacuum cleaner out along with the feather dusters and the polishing cloths and we tidied up *Staff Only*. While we were doing it, we heard the sound of Carter's Contract Cleaners arriving out in the alley. But we didn't bat an eyelid really and just carried on as if we were all part of the cleaning team. And when Marge the cleaner and the lady who wasn't Marge came along and found us there they weren't surprised at all.

Marge just waved to Mum and said, 'Hello love, how are you? Got the kids with you again. But they're no trouble are they? Bless them.' And then she patted little Angeline on the head. But when she wasn't looking, Angeline wiped the pat off.

Then the cleaning lady who wasn't Marge said, 'If you're doing the corridors, we'll go and do the staff canteen, same as before. Okay?'

'Okey dokey,' Mum agreed. And off Marge and the lady who wasn't Marge went, just like we were all part of the same cleaning team – which we were, as far they were concerned. They just thought we'd arrived in one of the other cleaning vans, or had maybe got there under our own steam.

So we pretended to be cleaners for a while and then kept out of the way until the real cleaners had gone. And we didn't just *pretend* to be cleaners, we did some good hard work too. We maybe couldn't sing for our suppers, but we could certainly polish for them.

Once the cleaners had driven off in their vans, we went to the staff showers for our nightly wash, and then we brushed our teeth and got into our pyjamas. I had a bit of homework to do, and Mum found a nice desk for me to do it at in Home Furnishings while she took Angeline up to TV and Electrical to watch the hundred tellies and to leave me in peace to concentrate.

Then, after seeing some cartoons, she put Angeline to bed in the tent down in Sports, Outdoors and Camping, and she soon fell asleep too, lulled by the sound of the ornamental fountain and the little artificial waterfall in Gardening, Garden Furniture and Tools.

Mum borrowed a baby listener then from Child and Nursery and she plugged it in near Angeline and took the handset with her and went off to Staff Services and Utilities to put our clothes in the washing machine. She told me that I could stay up a bit later than Angeline and that when I had finished my homework I could either read or watch a bit of telly or go on one of the computers. She said not to worry about Angeline as she had the handset and if she heard her wake up she'd go straight to her.

I decided to have a play on a computer, so Mum let me go up to the Faxes, Modems, Computers and Telecommunications Department (she said I was old enough to go alone and I promised not to break anything). I turned a computer on and got it going and I had a game of Hangman, Nibbles and Chomp and then I got the multimedia encyclopaedia going and had a look at that.

Mum came by a while later to see how I was getting on, and when I said I was okay, she said that she was going off to Fitness and Leisure in that case to have a go on the rowing machine, as she felt she needed the exercise and wanted to lose a bit of weight. So off she went and had half an hour on that.

When she returned, it was to tell me that it was bedtime; so I turned the computer off and we went down to Sports, Outdoors and Camping in the basement. Angeline was fast asleep inside our tent and she was gurgling too. But you really couldn't tell her gurgles from the gurgling of the fountain and the waterfall. I felt greatly reassured by that. I felt I would be able to sleep easier. I was confident now that when the watchman came on his middle-of-the-night patrol he would walk straight by us and never hear a thing.

I got into my sleeping bag then. Mum said she was going off to Staff Services and Utilities to see that the clothes were dry and to do some ironing, but that she'd take the baby listener handset with her and if there was any trouble I just had to call and she'd come running.

And so that was that.

I lay in my sleeping bag, listening to the gurgling going on around me, smelling the nice canvas smell of the tent. I felt secure and safe at last. It's funny how quickly you can make yourself at home in a place. A few hours ago I'd hated Scottley's. I'd dreaded going back there and had been terrified of us getting caught and found out and landing in awful trouble.

But now it was just like a home from home. We had our routine, we didn't bother anyone and they didn't bother us. And it was only for four weeks, after all. We could survive four weeks in Scottley's, couldn't we? It wasn't *that* long, the time would pass. Sundays would be the worst, because once we were inside the store we couldn't go out – except up on to the roof garden – without setting off the burglar alarms. But at least we did have the roof garden and we could survive one day a week inside, surely.

So I fell asleep, feeling warm and safe, feeling

that it was only a matter of time before everything worked out for the best.

You know, just for a while there, I actually stopped worrying. And I shouldn't have done. Because you can't afford to stop worrying, not for a moment, not with a mum like mine.

Yes, it was all going to be fine, I thought. The next four weeks would go by like clockwork and then we'd move into our own little house in Western Drive. What could be simpler or smoother?

But what did I know?

CHAPTER THIRTEEN

We followed the usual routine next morning and it was then the same routine every day. Wake up, dress, return the baby listener to Child and Nursery, pack everything into the big suitcase, hide the suitcase under a camp bed in one of the tents or put it behind one of the displays. Up to the Food Hall then to see if there were any sell-bys – especially any sell-by sandwiches that I could take to school with me for my lunch. Off to the staff canteen then to eat our breakfast. Wash everything up and then off to customer ladies' to play Hide in the Cubicle for half an hour until we could safely leave the store.

Hiding in the cubicle in customer ladies' was the most nerve-wracking bit of all. Especially when Miss Greystone and Mrs Gregg came in and went through their morning routine of:

'Customer ladies', Miss Greystone!'

'Customer ladies', Mrs Gregg!'

'Up to standard and Scottley-shape, Miss Greystone?'

'Clean and up to scratch, Mrs Gregg.'

'Kindly mark it in the book, Miss Greystone.'

'Kindly confirm that I have marked it in the book, Mrs Gregg.'

'Pleasure, Miss Greystone.'

'Thank you, Mrs Gregg.'

'On with the inspection, Miss Greystone.'

'Lead the way, Mrs Gregg!'

It was only when their stiletto heels had click-clacked away that I could breathe properly again. It was giving me asthma, all that tension. I was so frightened that one of us might sneeze or that one of us might fall off the toilet seat as we all stood there, clinging together in the cubicle, willing Miss Greystone and Mrs Gregg to get their inspection over with and go away. What if little Angeline should get the giggles? Or what if she should get tired of playing Hide in the Cubicle every morning and evening and suddenly have a tantrum while Miss Greystone and Mrs Gregg were standing just inches away on the other side of the door? What if one morning they decided to try the door handle and to look inside? My heart used to beat so loudly

I'm surprised they didn't hear it. It was awful. It was worse than being next in line to go bungee jumping, or waiting to have injections, I don't mind telling you.

The other stressful bit was going out and coming back into Scottley's. No matter which door we chose, Mr Whiskers always seemed to be there.

If we chose the front entrance, there he was; if we chose any one of half a dozen side entrances, there he was again. He saw us every morning and every night. He must have suspected something, I was sure of it from the way his whiskers bristled and seemed to turn up at the ends like bull horns every time we approached. And we were certainly a red rag to him. Just the sight of us coming down the corridor was enough to set his whiskers twitching. I knew that he thought we were up to something, he just couldn't think what it was – I hoped.

But there was nothing much he could do, was there? Although I think he did report us to a store detective once, as this man in a dark suit followed us all round the shop one evening and right into the cafeteria. He sat there at a nearby table, watching us as we had our drinks. But he was very obvious about it, not subtle at all.

We thought that he was never going to go away and that we wouldn't be able to hide in the customer ladies' that night; or if we did, he'd loiter about in the corridor outside, waiting for us to re-appear. I had visions of us being forced to leave the shop at five-thirty along with everyone else and maybe spending the night on a park bench. And we wouldn't even have our big suitcase, as that was down behind a radiator in Sports, Outdoors and Camping. And how could we go and retrieve it, with this horrible store detective dogging our footsteps every inch of the way just like his middle name was Fido?

But he must have decided we were harmless, as he went off in the end and followed somebody else. He trailed after a very posh-looking woman who seemed to have lots of lumpy bits under her coat, as if she'd been stuffing things up her jumper instead of paying for them. So we were able to hide in the customer ladies' as usual, and sleep down in our tent for yet another night.

One other thing which worried me was the security cameras. There were security cameras all over Scottley's, loads of them everywhere, all peering at you from every corner to make sure you didn't go pinching anything.

Now the cameras didn't really bother us at first, because although they were left on during the night, there was only the night-watchman to come along and look at the monitors – which you could see flickering at you from behind the glass panel of a door marked *Security*, down in the *Staff Only* section, not far from the canteen.

They didn't seem to video-record what the cameras saw though, but I had a feeling all that was about to change. Scottley's had been one of the first to install security cameras, but their system – once so advanced – was now very out of date. I had noticed workmen in the store wearing overalls marked *Video Surveillance Security Systems Ltd*, and they seemed to be changing all the security cameras, one by one, and replacing them with new ones. And sooner or later they'd install video-recorders and have it all on tape. And the tape was bound to record us and if anybody then took the trouble to play through what the cameras had recorded during the night, (which nobody probably bothered to do, unless there was a good reason, as it would have taken too long) there we'd be for all the world to see, getting into our tent in Sports, Camping and Outdoors and rummaging through the Food Hall looking for sell-bys.

So I just hoped that we'd be able to leave and move into our house before the new security system was up and running. But it was one more thing to worry about. Yes, it certainly was. And every night I was careful to peer into the office marked *Security* to see if the new video-tape machines had been installed yet or not.

And you know something, I wasn't the only person wondering about that. I wasn't the only person in the shop keeping an eye on the new security cameras.

On Friday, when there was late-night shopping and the store didn't close until eight, we went off to the cinema after Mum and Angeline had picked me up from school, so as to have something to do to pass the time. Mum had managed to get a part-time job during the day, helping out in a health food shop where she had worked once before. So she was kept busy while Angeline was at nursery and I was at school.

By the time we left the cinema and finally got to Scottley's, it was seven-forty and little Angeline was yawning something terrible.

Please don't let Mr Whiskers be at the door. I prayed.

Please don't let us see Mr Whiskers. Just for once let him not be there.

We chose an insignificant-looking side door, one that didn't get much use because all the rich and important customers liked to go to the front entrance where everyone could see them and where Mr Whiskers or one of the other doormen would bow and say, 'How nice to see you again, modom. Such a pleasure to have you back, sir.'

Some of the customers even arrived in Rolls Royces driven by their chauffeurs. And the chauffeurs sat out there, waiting in the cars, parked on the double yellow lines where they had no right to be. But they didn't care. And not even the traffic wardens could get them to move. Even when the traffic wardens gave them parking tickets they didn't budge. They'd just say, 'The modom I work for has so much money that she cares not a bit for parking tickets. She gives not a hoot for them. The fines for parking tickets are no more than small change and pocket money to her. Modom spends more than that on taking her false eye-lashes to the laundry. Yes, modom has given me instructions to wait right here. So I will, even if you paper the entire windscreen with parking tickets. We shall not be moved. Modom says so.'

And you got the feeling that not even the most ferocious traffic warden was half as frightening as modom.

So the chauffeurs would stay right where they were. Sometimes they'd even rip the parking tickets up, right in front of the traffic warden, and then stick the bits in his top pocket. Which used to make him pretty mad, as you can imagine.

Mr Whiskers never said, 'How nice to see you again, modoms,' to us though. The most he ever said to us was, 'Oh no, not you lot!', which I thought was pretty rude really, considering what regular customers we were. Not that we spent much money in Scottley's, but it was like our second home. Well, our first home really. Well, our only home at that moment. And we did look after the place and do a bit of cleaning every night, which was more than he did. He just stood there growing his moustache and whistling at taxis.

So anyway, we went to the small side entrance, hoping that we could slip into the store without having to meet up with those ferocious whiskers again. The coast seemed clear . . . we pushed the door open . . . in we went and—

What should we see but one huge great

moustache. It was just like there was a big sabre-toothed walrus lying in wait for us. Yes, it was Mr Whiskers in person. There he was again. He looked about as surprised to see us as we did to see him. And you know what I think he was doing? I think he was on the skive. I think he'd got fed-up whistling for taxis and opening doors and saying, 'Nice to see you again, modom,' and he'd come down to this quiet side door for a bit of a rest.

Well, when he saw us his mouth fell open like the boot of a car.

'No!' he said. 'I don't *believe* it! *You lot*! Here *again*! You're always here! You practically live in the place.'

'As a matter of fact,' little Angeline began to say, 'we—'

But I managed to get a toffee into her mouth just in time before she managed to say any more.

'Thanks, Livvy,' she chewed. (It was my only toffee too, but I didn't grudge it to her. It was worth it.)

He stood right in front of us, blocking our way with his great whiskers. His shoulders were broad, but his whiskers were even broader and they all but filled the doorway.

'Now look here, you lot,' he said. 'I don't know

what your game is, but I have my suspicions. And if I ever catch you doing – whatever it is you are doing – I'll have you banned.'

'Oh will you indeed, my man!' Mum said, going into hoity-toity mode again (and she could be very good at hoity-toity when she wanted to, for all her itchy feet and the gypsy in her soul). 'Well, let me tell you that we are among Scottley's most regular customers!'

'Well, I never see you buying anything,' Mr Whiskers said. 'I never see you coming out with any bags.'

'That,' Mum said, 'is because we have it all delivered. We buy so much we couldn't possibly carry it all, so we have it sent round to us in a truck. A very large truck as well, I might add. Sometimes even *two* trucks! Two trucks and a van! And a bicycle.'

Mr Whiskers gave her a twitchy look, as if he didn't know whether to believe her or not.

'One word from me,' Mum warned him, 'and you would be instantly dismissed.'

'Oh *would* I now!' Mr Whiskers said. And I could see that Mum had maybe gone a bit too far.

'Yes,' Mum went on. 'Because doormen are easy enough to find, even ones with large whiskers.

Because if they haven't got large whiskers to start with, they can always grow some. Unless they're ladies, of course. But even then, they could get some stick-on ones from the Jokes, Pranks and Novelties Department. But regular, high-spending customers with deep handbags and more money than they know what to do with are more like needles in haystacks.'

'Yes,' Mr Whiskers growled, 'I reckon they are. But I don't reckon you lot are needles. You look more like hay to me. Or possibly even straw.'

'How rude!' Mum said indignantly. 'I've half a mind to take my business elsewhere.'

'Oh would you?' Mr Whiskers said, 'I'd be so grateful.'

'I don't think you would,' Mum said. 'And I don't think that Scottley's management would be very pleased to hear that one of their most regular customers had been driven away to shop elsewhere thanks to the surly attitude of their doorman.'

Mr Whiskers gave her a very long hard stare.

'I've got my eye on you,' he said again. 'I most definitely have got my eye on you lot. And I'll be keeping my eye on you until I find out what you're up to. You're always arriving just as we're about to close, and you're always coming out a few minutes after we've opened. So you're up to something. I know that. I haven't quite worked out what it is yet, but I will, don't you worry. I'm going to get myself a pen and a piece of paper when I go home tonight, and I'm going to write all the facts down, and I'm going to put two and two together and work out what you're up to. You see if I don't. And then there'll be trouble – in three different sizes to suit each one of you. Small trouble,' he said, nodding at Angeline, 'medium trouble,' and he nodded at me, 'and grown-up trouble.'

And we all knew who the grown-up trouble was for.

But Mum wasn't bothered in the least.

'Stand aside, my man,' she commanded, 'and permit us ladies to enter our favourite store, or I shall have to report you to the manger, who is a personal friend.' (Well, he was bound to be a personal friend of somebody. And Mum never said he was *her* personal friend, did she?)

So Mr Whiskers reluctantly stood aside and let us go on into the shop. He wasn't at all pleased about it though and as we disappeared inside I heard him muttering to himself.

'Go in just before closing time, come out just after we open up? Hmm. Definitely something going on there. Only *what*? What *are* they up to?'

And I glanced back to see him chewing away at one of the ends of his moustache, just like a horse with a nosebag.

It was ages before we got to bed that Friday, what with the late-night opening and all. The shop didn't close until eight, which meant that dinner was late and we had terrible trouble finding a sell-by to eat, as most of the stuff had gone from the Food Hall, almost as if the place had been invaded by locusts.

Then, of course, the cleaners would be coming round too – and later than ever as well. It was nine o'clock when we heard their vans arriving out in the alleyway and by then poor little Angeline was about dead on her feet.

'Mum,' I said, 'do we have to pretend to be cleaners again tonight? Can't we just go to sleep in our tent down in Sports, Outdoors and Camping? I mean, if the security guard walks past us every night and never sees us – well, it's not very likely that the cleaners are going to notice us either, is it? I know it means we'll miss our shower in *Staff*

Only, but that won't matter just for one night, will it? Little Angeline looks so tired and so am I, to tell the truth.'

'All right,' Mum agreed. 'I'll just brush your teeth quickly in customer ladies'.'

So she did and then Angeline and I hurried down to Sports, Outdoors and Camping and got into our sleeping bags inside our tent.

I thought that Mum would have an early night too, but she said that she had better go and pretend to be a cleaner as well, otherwise the real cleaners might get suspicious and wonder where she was. And besides she had some things to pay for by working them off.

To be honest though, I don't think those were the real reasons. I think she just wanted to have a chat with Marge and the lady who wasn't Marge. I think she quite liked talking to them and I could imagine them saying to her, 'Not got the littl'uns with you tonight?' And Mum answering, 'No, they're safely tucked up at home tonight,' never mentioning that home was a tent and a sleeping bag down in Sports, Outdoors and Camping.

Little Angeline fell asleep almost immediately, but I stayed awake for a while, listening to the ornamental waterfall and the tinkling fountain over in Gardening, Garden Furniture and Tools. It was just like the country, when you closed your eyes. You could almost hear the birds singing – not that birds do sing at night, of course . . . well, not many of them anyway. Just nightingales and nightjars maybe, or so I've read. Not that I've ever heard them.

And you know, as I lay there, it occurred to me that in just the same way that Mr Whiskers kept seeing us, there was someone *I* kept seeing in Scottley's and I'd never really bothered about it before. But the more I thought about it, the more I kept seeing this man in my mind's eye. I realised that we saw him at least once a day and he was always more or less in the same place, strolling through the Perfumery Department just like he was looking for a present for a lady, or maybe thinking of getting some after-shave for himself. If he wasn't there, he'd be admiring the displays of necklaces, gold watches and rings in the Jewellery and Precious Stones section. He seemed to have plenty of money to spend and he was always dead smart and wore a posh overcoat.

I wondered if maybe he was a store detective, but then I thought no, he seemed too well-off for that. Not unless Scottley's had given him the overcoat to wear, of course, just so that he could blend in with the shoppers and so that people wouldn't think that he was a store detective at all. I supposed that might have been possible and yet I somehow didn't feel it was so.

So if he wasn't a store detective, who was he? What was he doing there? Why did I keep seeing him? Because you never really saw him buying anything and he never seemed to stay anywhere that long. He just seemed to be always browsing around.

Then I remembered that I'd seen him somewhere else too. I'd seen him going through one of the doors marked *Staff Only*. But a few moments later he'd come out again, just as if he'd gone in there by accident and it was all a silly mistake. And then one other time I'd seen him up on the top floor and he was talking to one of the assistants and asking her about the roof garden and whether it was open to the public, and she'd said no, not at the moment, but it might be later on in the summer. He'd smiled and thanked her and had been about to go on his way when he turned and saw me watching him.

And you know what he did?

He winked!

Just like he knew all about us. Just as if he knew that we were living in a tent down in Sports, Outdoors and Camping. And yet he couldn't have known that, could he? Or he'd have told somebody and had us thrown out and got us into all sorts of trouble.

Yes, he winked and then he sailed off down the escalator. It was very odd really, all very mysterious. So mysterious in fact that I decided that this was what I would call him – Mr Mysterious. There was Mr Whiskers, the doorman, and now there was Mr Mysterious, the customer with the wonderful overcoat, who looked very rich but who never bought anything.

I wondered for a moment if he could have been my dad, back from the oil rigs with loads of money, and if he was looking for us in all the shops. Maybe he'd winked because he'd recognised me. But no. No, he wouldn't have just left it at that; he'd have said something. You don't just wink at your long lost daughter who you haven't seen for years. You at least stop and talk to her and ask how she's been getting on at school. You don't leave it at winking, you'd need to do a bit better than that.

As I dropped off to sleep, my last thoughts were of Mr Mysterious and who he might be. I made a mental note to ask Mum if she had noticed him at all, and I resolved to keep a look-out for him tomorrow and see if he would be there again. And then my eyes closed and I fell into a deep, deep sleep, and when I opened them again it was to complete and utter confusion.

Mum was leaning over me and shaking me for all she was worth.

'Livvy!' she said in a sharp whisper, 'Livvy, Livvy! Come on, wake up, quickly! Wake up!'

I opened my eyes and looked at her, and for the first time in ages I saw that she was actually worried about something. More than worried; she was in a state of panic.

'Livvy!' she said. 'Livvy, something terrible's happened!'

I immediately sat up in my sleeping bag.

'What Mum? Is it Angeline? Is she ill? Is she okay?'

'No, it's not that,' Mum said. 'It's not that. But it's almost as bad.'

'What, Mum, *what*?'

'Look,' she said, and she held one of the alarm clocks she had borrowed from Clocks and Watches up to my nose. 'I forgot to set the alarm last night. We've slept in! We've overslept, Livvy. Look at the time! It's *twenty-five past eight*. The staff must already be here. In another five minutes the customers will be coming in. And we're all still in our pyjamas in the tent. How are we going to get out? We're stuck, stuck in the tent in the Camping and Outdoors Department. What if somebody comes and looks inside? How do we get out without being seen! Oh, Livvy, *what are we going to do?'*

And I felt a sudden pang of fear and I needed to go to the toilet – in a hurry.

CHAPTER FOURTEEN

So there we were. Me, Mum, and a still-sleeping Angeline, all in our tent in Scottley's Sports, Outdoors and Camping Department at nearly half past eight on a Saturday morning, with the staff outside getting everything ready and the doors about to open and the customers about to pour in.

I listened. I could hear the shop assistants talking to each other, out on the other side of the canvas. They seemed to be some distance away, at the far end of the floor. If we kept our voices down to whispers, they probably wouldn't hear us. But how long could we stay in the tent for? Not for much longer, surely? Not when I needed the loo. And when little Angeline woke, she'd want the loo as well and her breakfast.

'Maybe we *can* just stay here all day,' Mum whispered to me. 'Stay here in the tent until they close at six tonight. It's only a few hours.'

A few hours! I almost yelled. Half past eight in the morning until six o'clock at night! Some few hours that was. It was (it took me a little while to work it out in my head, but I managed) nine and a half hours. Five hundred and seventy minutes!

Nine and a half hours! In a tent! In Scottley's! With nothing to eat or drink! With nothing to look at and nothing to read. Unable to talk or to move! And worst of all – with no toilet!

Nine and a half hours! It would be unbearable. And how was little Angeline going to lie still and be quiet for nine and a half hours? She had a hard job sitting still for nine and a half seconds. Maybe if we didn't disturb her she might go on sleeping until six o'clock. But I didn't think it too likely. And even if she did, even if we all could keep quiet and stay still and not make a sound and not go to the toilet until six o'clock in the evening, what if somebody came into the tent?

Saturday was a big shopping day, after all. It was when people took their families out and went to buy things like tents and TVs and kitchen tables. You'd see them endlessly arguing over which was the best, and one person would want one thing and another person would want another.

And you certainly wouldn't buy a tent without

looking inside it, would you? So if anyone took a fancy to our tent, they were bound to come in. Absolutely *bound* to.

Little Angeline began to make about-to-wake-up gurgles. She has several different kinds of gurgles and when you get to know them you can generally tell what's going to happen next.

'Shhh, Angel,' Mum whispered. 'Don't wake yet. Go on sleeping,' and she smoothed her hair, almost as if doing so might hypnotise her into snoozing on until six o'clock. She'd probably have put a spell on her too, if she'd known any.

'Mum,' I said quietly, 'I think I need to go to—'

'I *know*,' she snapped back, not even letting me finish, 'so do I.'

Yes and so will Angeline, I thought, *when she wakes up*. And the Outdoors Department of Scottley's wasn't like the real outdoors. You couldn't go digging a hole in the ground for a latrine or anything like that.

Little Angeline gurgled again and squirmed around in her sleeping bag. The assistants' voices were nearer and louder now. They weren't far from our tent. Then there was another voice, then more voices. The first customers of the day had arrived, all ready, willing and eager to spend their money.

'Yes, madam? Yes, sir?' one of the assistants said. 'Can I help you at all?'

Please, I thought to myself, *please say that all you want to buy is a camping stove or a spare mallet to hammer your tent pegs in. Whatever you do, don't say that you've come to buy—*

'We've come to buy a tent,' a man's voice announced. 'We've decided we've had enough of hotels and apartments. It's an outdoor holiday for us next year. So we got here bright and early – the whole family – got here before the crowds. Beat the rush, you know, and we need something to suit the four of us. Don't we, eh?'

'Yes, Dad', two voices said. They were boys' voices. One of them sounded about my age and the other about Angeline's.

Angeline gurgled again and tossed about in her sleeping bag. She was about to wake up at any moment. And then, of course, as soon as she woke up—

Oh no! She'd start *singing*! She would. That was her new habit. That was the latest thing. She'd start singing at the top of her voice. That song she'd heard on the radio, *Oh, What A Beautiful Morning*. Even when it was a horrible morning she still sang it. Oh no, oh no, oh –

Angeline's eyes flickered open.

'Oh, what a beaut—'

I just got my hand over her mouth in time before her voice got any louder.

'I'm sorry,' I heard the assistant say from outside the tent, 'Did you say something?'

'Me? No,' the man said. 'Probably the boys messing about. So it's all right if we take a look at the tents, is it? Crawl around in them, peer inside, all that?'

'Oh, of course, sir. Please feel free. And if you need any other help or information, I'll be just over there by the till.'

'Right,' the man said. 'Thanks very much. We'll have a look around and give you a shout.'

Angeline's eyes were swimming round in her head like goldfish in a bowl. I knew if I didn't take my hand away soon she'd bite it. I leaned over and put my mouth right next to her ear.

'Angeline,' I whispered, 'I'm sorry I had to put my hand over your mouth, but we're in big trouble. We've slept in late and the shop's open. We must be very quiet so that no one knows we're in here. So I'll take my hand off now but you've got to be very, very quiet, okay? Whispers only. Silence if possible. Okay? Don't start singing *Oh*,

What A Beautiful Morning whatever you do. Do you understand? I'm going to take my hand off now. Okay?'

She nodded. I removed my hand.

'Livvy,' she whispered in a very small voice.

'Yes?'

'I need to go to—'

'I know,' I said. 'We all do.'

'Yes, but I *really* need to go.'

'I *know*,' I said. 'So do I.'

I looked at Mum. *Well, Mum*, I thought, *now what? See, this is where all your no-worries gets you, slap bang into the middle of a big load of trouble. And just how do we get out of this one?*

It wasn't as if we could have dashed out of the tent and made a run for it, either. Not only were we in our sleeping bags, we were still in our pyjamas. We could hardly grab our big suitcase and go running through the store and out into the street in pyjamas. We'd definitely have been arrested then and no mistake. (Well, we have been arrested, haven't we, I suppose, more or less?)

On the other side of the canvas I could hear those people talking to each other. They must have been looking at the big frame tent first, because the man said, 'This looks all right,' to which the woman said, 'Have you seen the price of it? And anyway, it's too big.' To which the smallest boy said, '*I* like it,' to which his bigger brother said, 'Well, I don't and I'm never sleeping in that!' to which his brother said, 'Well you can sleep in the dustbin then, can't you?'

Then it sounded as if some kind of fight had started because their dad said, 'Boys, boys! Stop that!' in a very loud booming voice and their mother said. 'It's disgraceful, you can't take them anywhere. And if you do, you have to go back afterwards to apologise and pay for all the damage.'

Our mum took advantage of the noise and commotion to hand us our clothes and to indicate that we were to get dressed, but that on no account were we to bump against the sides of the tent and so give ourselves away.

We wriggled and squirmed out of our pyjamas and wriggled and squirmed into our clothes, and all the while the people outside were getting nearer and nearer to our tent.

'Here's one that looks like an igloo,' I heard the older of the two boys say. 'Can we go inside, Dad?'

'The shop assistant said it was all right, so I should think so, yes.'

I could map their progress in my mind. They'd go inside the igloo tent and they'd go inside the tent next to it and then they'd both try to get inside the one-man tent, specially designed for Arctic explorers. Then, when they'd finished fighting about that, they'd want to get inside the tent next to it – the one that had no posts and which you blew up with a foot-pump. And then they'd be at our tent and they'd want to go inside that too. And we'd be there, half-in and half-out of our pyjamas, all desperately needing to go to the toilet.

'Hurry,' Mum mouthed, 'hurry, hurry, hurry!'

I'd put my knickers on back to front. But never mind, I'd just have to put up with it. There wasn't the time to take them off and put them back on again the right way round.

Mum finished getting herself dressed, then she helped Angeline. She put our pyjamas away in the big suitcase, which had been under her bed, and she helped us on with our shoes. She gathered up all our other bits and pieces and stuffed them untidily into the case on top of the pyjamas. Then she handed us our outdoor coats and nodded at us to put them on.

'Mum, I really need to go to—' Angeline whispered, and Mum mouthed 'I know,' and

216

'just try to hold on a moment.'

She closed the case and locked it, her thumbs pushing the catches softly into place so as not to make a sound.

'Right,' she whispered. 'We're ready.'

I looked at her blankly. What did she mean, *ready*? Ready for *what*? The people out there were getting nearer and nearer. Any second they'd be right by our tent. They'd be looking at it from the outside and admiring it, saying what a nice colour it was and what a good, practical design – all the reasons why we'd chosen to sleep in it. And then they'd be yanking at the tent flap, sliding the zip on the door open, to pull back the sides and reveal – *us*.

And then what?

Disaster! What else?

I glanced at Mum. But she didn't look worried any more. In fact she seemed to be smiling, almost laughing even. Well, I couldn't see what was so funny. Here we were in one of the worst predicaments she'd ever got us into, and all she could do was to sit there grinning about it. Well, I didn't see –

'Listen, you two,' Mum whispered. 'Whatever I say, just agree with it? Okay?'

'But Mum—'

'Shhh, Livvy. Trust me. Just agree with me. Please.'

And she motioned me to be quiet and not to argue any more.

They were outside. Standing right next to us. The little boy's hand pushed against the canvas sides of the tent.

'Feels nice,' he said.

Little Angeline raised her hand to touch his from our side of the canvas. I reached up and took her hand before she could do so. She thought I was just being friendly and she smiled.

'Shall we have a look inside?' the man's voice said. 'See if it's as cosy on the inside as it seems to be on the out?'

'Good idea,' the woman said. 'I rather like the look of this one. Don't you, Tim?'

'Not bad, I suppose,' the bigger boy's voice reluctantly agreed.

Next I saw the shadow of a large hand approach the tent flap, reaching for the zip so as to pull it up and to open the tent door and . . .

But before the hand could get to the zip from the outside, Mum got to it from the inside.

She yanked the zip right open, threw the tent flaps back, stood up – to the complete and utter astonishment of the four people there – picked up our suitcase and said, 'No, I don't think so girls. It's a very nice tent, but not quite right for our requirements. Let's go and have a look at a few more.'

And she led us out of the tent; straight past the lady, the man and the two boys, who stood there gawping at us, as if they couldn't believe their own eyes.

Mum gave them one of her big smiles.

'So difficult, isn't it, deciding on a tent?' she said. 'Hard to find something that everyone likes. In fact, girls,' she said to us, 'perhaps we should have a break from looking at tents and go to the cafeteria instead.'

I didn't care where we went just so long as we passed a customer ladies' on the way. So off we strode: Mum at the front with the big suitcase, then me and little Angeline following her (and me feeling a bit uncomfortable because of my back-to-front knickers).

I looked back at the family. They were still standing gawping, and I saw the man turn to the lady and heard her say, 'However did they come out of there? I never saw them going in?'

I also noticed the shop assistant glance up at us with a rather puzzled expression on his face as we traipsed past the till. He was plainly wondering how and when we'd come into the department and why he hadn't seen us. But Mum just gave him one of her friendly, reassuring smiles and said, 'Thank you very much. We'll maybe come back later for another look. It'll give us a chance to think things over and make up our minds.'

'Oh, yes, of course, madam, thank you very much,' the assistant said. He probably thought that he had been busy with his head down over his paperwork and computer printouts when we had arrived. 'Would you like to take a few leaflets?' he asked. 'And a price list?'

'Right you are,' Mum said. 'Thank you very much.' And she swept out of the Sports, Camping and Outdoors Department as grandly as she could – and she can be very grand when she wants to.

Angeline and I followed her, trying to be grand as well, walking with our heads held high – even though we were desperate for the loo (or possibly because we were desperate for the loo). And if the assistant did stop to wonder what Mum was doing with a great big suitcase in her hand at that time of the morning, he didn't have the nerve to ask. He just watched silently as we disappeared up the escalator, just like we were saints going up to heaven.

We went straight to the nearest customer ladies' and I was able to sort my knickers out. You can't imagine how uncomfortable it was having them on back to front, not unless you've done the same yourself. Then we washed our hands and faces and Mum said she'd buy us breakfast in the cafeteria.

'What about the sell-bys?' little Angeline asked in a rather too loud voice.

'Sell-bys are just for when we're on our own,' Mum explained. 'Not for when the shop's full of people.'

'Have we got enough money for breakfast?' I asked, worrying, as usual.

'Oh yes,' Mum said. 'I try not to spend it if we don't have to. But yes, I think we've enough for some food. But first, I must get rid of this case.'

She looked around for somewhere to leave the suitcase.

There was a small broom cupboard there inside customer ladies', so she opened the door and hid the suitcase in there, behind some buckets and squeegee mops.

'We'll get it later,' she said. 'When we come back tonight.'

Back tonight. Another night, then another and another. Another three weeks in Scottley's before we could move into our new house in Western Drive. I didn't think my nerves could stand it. I'd probably have a mental breakdown by Thursday at the latest.

Even though it was still quite early in the day, the store was already crowded. There were Saturday shoppers spilling in through all the doors, and I bet myself that Mr Whiskers must have been tipping his hat and whistling himself silly trying to get taxis. He'd give himself a sore throat with all his 'sirs' and 'modoms'.

We weren't the first customers in the cafeteria either; there were already half a dozen or so there, most of them having breakfast. There was bacon frying and sausages sizzling and eggs bubbling and toast turning golden brown. We all ate a big, hearty breakfast each, just as if we were celebrating our first week of living in Scottley's. *If only*, I thought, *it would be our last week too*.

And little did I know that it would be.

* * *

Now, I'll tell you a funny thing, while I remember it; it was somebody I saw come into the cafeteria. He wasn't wearing his beautiful overcoat, so I didn't recognise him at first. But I knew there was something familiar about him the moment he walked past our table and went up to the counter to get himself a tray. It was Mr Mysterious. Yes, Mr Mysterious again. And when I saw him there, I thought to myself, *What if he's living in the store too?* What if it wasn't even his overcoat and he'd just borrowed it from Suits, Jackets and Trousers, the same way little Angeline had borrowed the big doll from the Toy Department, not in order to steal it or to keep it, but just to enjoy it for a little while and then to put it back.

Yes, what if Mr Mysterious was living in Scottley's too? Maybe he hid every night at closing time in a cubicle in customer gents'. Then, when the store was empty, he crept out to sleep in a big trunk in Luggage and Travel, just like a vampire in a plush-lined coffin. Maybe he too was waiting for a house to fall vacant in Western Drive? But if he *was* living in the store, it was funny our paths hadn't crossed. But then again, Scottley's was a big place and you could easily walk around it for days and not meet the same person twice.

And then, you know, as I sat there poking a toast soldier into the yolk of my boiled egg, I began to have this wonderful fantasy. It was all about Mum and Mr Mysterious and how Mum would get a letter from Dad out on the oil rigs saying that he wouldn't be able to come home any more as he had fallen in love with this Arab sheikh's beautiful daughter. He'd say how sorry he was, but he hoped that Mum wouldn't mind too much as they hadn't seen each other for years and years anyway. And Mum would be a bit sad at first, but not for long, and then she'd be free to marry somebody else, like Mr Mysterious. Maybe they'd meet in Scottley's, in the Glass, China and Homeware Department one evening, and it would be love at first sight, and we could all move into the new house in Western Drive together and be happy ever after, like in the fairy tales.

Because you know, he was a very handsome man, was Mr Mysterious. Almost like a film star. He really did look like somebody special (and he was too, in his fashion; only not, as it turned out, quite in the way I thought).

I tried to draw Mum's attention to him, to get her a bit interested.

'There's that man again, Mum,' I said, giving her elbow a nudge as she spooned in her cornflakes.

'Don't jog me,' she said, 'you'll spill it.'

'But it's that man,' I said. 'He's here. In the cafeteria.'

'Which man?'

'The one I keep seeing, the one I told you about. The one with the overcoat.'

'I don't see anyone with an overcoat.'

'No, he's not wearing it today, that's why I didn't recognise him at first. There he is, over there. I keep seeing him all the time, down in Perfumery, and he seems very interested in Jewellery and Precious Stones as well. Him. There. That's the one.'

Mum was plainly worried about this man. If we kept seeing him that might well mean that *he* kept seeing *us*. She swivelled in her chair and glanced round at him.

Let it be love at first sight, I prayed. *Please let it be real true everlasting love at first sight.*

But it wasn't. I mean, she seemed interested in him, but only in a suspicious way.

'Probably a floor-walker,' Mum said.

'What's a floor-walker, Mum?' little Angeline

asked, her mouth full of toast and honey.

'Some one who walks on floors, of course!' I snapped at her, feeling at bit irritable because my love-at-first-sight idea hadn't gone to plan.

'Can he walk on ceilings too?' Angeline asked, with no idea at all that I'd just been nasty to her, which made me even more annoyed, because what's the good in being rude to people if they can't appreciate it? You're just wasting your breath. 'Can he walk on walls too?' she went on. 'Can he walk on windows? Is there anything else he can walk on? Can you ask him to come over here and walk on the table? Can he do handstands?'

'No, floor-walker is another way of saying store detective, Angeline,' Mum explained.

'What's a store detective?' Angeline asked, just like I knew she would. We'd be there all morning now while one explanation led to yet another question. You felt you were going round in circles sometimes when she got like that.

'It's a person responsible for shop security,' Mum said.

'What's security?' Angeline asked.

'You know, stopping stealing and shoplifting and that.'

'What's shoplifting?' she said. 'How can you lift a shop, Mum? Shops are too big to lift, aren't they?' (We were going to be at it for hours. She'd only just got started.)

'You could use a crane, Angeline,' I said.

'What's a crane?'

I gave up and let Mum handle it.

'Your toast is getting cold, Angeline,' she said, trying to distract her.

And that seemed to do the trick. She stopped asking questions then and went back to her breakfast.

'Don't you think he's handsome, Mum?' I said. 'Mr Mysterious over there.?'

Mum took another look at him.

'In his way, I suppose.' she said. 'Not one that would appeal to me though.'

'You might get to like him if you knew him better,' I said.

'I don't want to know him better, thank you very much. As long as I know that he's not a store detective and that he's not got his eye on us, that'll do for me.'

So much for my dreams and fantasies. So much for us all living together in a house in Western Drive and being happy ever after. I thought it was pretty selfish of Mum really, not falling in love at first sight like she was supposed to, especially when I'd gone to all the trouble of finding someone nice for her. But there you are. There's no pleasing some people – least of all your own family. I don't think you get more self-centred people than your own relations. I mean, all she had to do was marry him. I wasn't expecting that much. It wasn't as if I was asking for a bike.

'Shall we go and watch all the tellies now?' little Angeline asked, when she could eat no more toast. 'Might be cartoons on.'

'No, I don't think so,' Mum said. 'TV, Radio and Electrical will probably be rather busy on a Saturday; it might be best if we went out for a while.'

'But that's not fair,' Angeline wailed. 'Not fair that other people should come in and watch *our* tellies. We *live* here. This is our home. We don't go round to *their* homes and watch *their* tellies, do we? Not right, Mum.'

'Yes, well, other people don't live in department stores though, Angeline. That does make a slight difference.'

But, 'Huh!' was all Angeline would say, 'Not fair!'

Just then, to make matters worse, a woman came into the cafeteria along with her daughter, a little girl of about Angeline's age. And in her arms she was carrying a Miss Daisy doll – the same as the display one which Angeline had borrowed from the Toy Department, the one which slept with its eyes open and wet its knickers. Angeline took one look at it, leapt to her feet, pointed and yelled at the top of her voice, 'THAT GIRL'S STOLEN MY DOLL!'

Mum went purple with embarrassment, and it takes a lot to embarrass *her*, I can tell you. You've normally more chance of making a rhino blush than my mum.

'Angeline! Be quiet!' she said.

But Angeline was already climbing up on to the cafeteria chair, just like someone getting up on to a platform to give a speech.

'That doll's not for taking away!' she yelled. 'It's only for borrowing and you have to put it back after! You're not allowed to carry it round during the day or people might find out that you're living in a tent!'

Mum picked Angeline up, wiped toast crumbs

from her with a napkin, put her down and said, 'Come on, girls, time to go, we've finished breakfast.'

'That girl's pinching things!' Angeline screeched. 'Get a store detective. She's doll-lifting! Get a carpet-walker.'

'Floor-walker!' I corrected her.

'Yes,' she said, 'get one of those as well! Go on, Livvy. Do something.'

Mum pushed us out of the cafeteria. Everyone was staring now. The little girl's mother looked really angry, while the girl herself was close to tears.

'I didn't steal the doll,' she wailed. 'Didn't steal it. Mum bought it for my birthday! *Waaaah!*'

'Stop, thief!' little Angeline shouted, as Mum tried to drag her away. 'There's a girl here lifting the shop! She's stealing all the dolls and she's not doing any cleaning to pay for them either. Look at it! It's not even a sell-by. She can't have it. It's not past its sell-by date!'

Mum was the colour of a postbox by now.

'I'm ever so sorry,' she stammered to the girl's mother. 'I must apologise for my daughter's behaviour. I can't think what's got into her. She's probably just jealous.'

But little Angeline heard her.

'Am not!' she wailed. 'I am not jealous! I'm just trying to stop all the pinching! It's not fair! If other people can pinch things, why can't I?'

'This way, Angel,' Mum said, practically putting little Angeline under her arm and carrying her out of the cafeteria. 'This way, dear. I think we all need some fresh air.'

'We don't,' Angeline cried. 'We need the police.'

And she started to cry.

CHAPTER FIFTEEN

By the time we got down all the escalators to the ground floor, Angeline's tears had stopped and she seemed to have forgotten all about the girl and the Miss Daisy doll and she was her usual, cheerful self again.

'Okay,' Mum said. 'Let's go out of the side door on the east wing. That doorman was there yesterday and they usually move him around. I can't see him being at the same entrance two days running. That seems to be the rule.'

So off we went to the small side door on the east wing. But sure enough, just as we turned the corner out from Sewing Machines and Haberdashery, who should we see but the very person we were trying to avoid – Mr Whiskers himself.

'No!' I heard Mum mutter, and she halted in her tracks. Angeline and I stopped too. He hadn't seen us yet. His back was towards us and he was facing the door. You could still see his whiskers though, poking out and curling up at either side of his head.

'Let's go out another way,' Mum said in a whisper, sort of miming and gesturing to get the message across.

We understood her and we quietly began to turn around . . . when Mr Whiskers went and turned round too. And he saw us.

'Oh, no!' he said. 'You lot! Not you lot again!'

There was no turning back now. To turn back would have made us seem guilty and as if we had something to hide (which we did, of course). But when you have something to hide and you don't want people thinking that, the best way is to pretend that you've got nothing to hide at all.

'Come on, girls,' Mum said. 'Let's be on our way.'

We strode on towards the door. Mr Whiskers looked down at us, his ferocious whiskers all a-tremble. We got to the door. I waited for Mum to open it. But she didn't. She stopped. She stood and looked at Mr Whiskers.

'Well?' he said.

'Well?' Mum said.

'Well, what?' he said.

'The door,' Mum said.

'Well, what about the door?' Mr Whiskers said.

'Yes, what about the door?' Mum said.

'What about what about the door?' Mr Whiskers said.

'Well?' Mum said. 'Aren't you going to open it for us?'

He went a most peculiar colour. It wasn't white; it wasn't grey; it was more a kind of sickly yellow, and his whiskers started to wave up and down like a bird flapping its wings. It made you think that his head might fly clean off his shoulders into Scottley's and just leave him there headless and whiskerless by the door.

At last he managed to speak.

'Open . . .' he spluttered 'the door . . . for *you lot*?'

'Please,' Mum said, with a sweet smile. 'If you wouldn't mind. You are the doorman, after all.'

'Well, of all the – – – –'

And then he just sort of gave up. Because, it was true, he was the doorman, wasn't he? And that was his job, opening and closing the doors for people and whistling up taxis and saying, 'Nice to see you, modom.'

So Mum was only really asking him to treat us

the same as he treated everyone else, wasn't she? She was only really asking him to do what he was paid for.

And you know what he did?

It was such a surprise. Because I thought for a moment there that he was going to pick us all up, one by one, and squash our heads in the door. But he didn't. Not a bit of it. You know what he did? He started to shake. His great broad shoulders began to tremble and the great whiskers started to vibrate. At first I thought he was crying, maybe having one of those mental breakdowns that I'd been thinking of having myself.

But no. He was laughing. Actually *laughing*! And he laughed so much that tears came into his eyes, and a few of them dropped onto the enormous whiskers and they worked their way along to the ends and fell off on to the floor, just like it was raining.

'Dear, oh, dear,' he gasped. 'Dear, oh, dear! Open the door! For you lot! That's a good one. That really is! Pardon me, but that really is a good one. My, oh, my. That really is.'

But that wasn't the end of it. There were even more surprises to come. Because what I expected him to say next was something like, 'Not on your

Nelly! Never in a million years! Not over my dead body will I open that door for you lot!' (Not that he could if he was dead, of course; not strictly speaking.)

But no. He opened the door.

Yes, it's true, he really did. He opened the door. He actually held the door open for us and he gave us this great, enormous smile and he pointed to little Angeline and he said, 'You first, modom.'

And little Angeline smiled right back, just as if she had enormous whiskers too, and she swanked right out of the door, as if she was Scottley's best and most valued customer. I went out next and then Mum came last.

Thank you, 'she said. 'Thank you very much.'

'Not at all,' Mr Whiskers said. 'My pleasure – *modom.*'

And he gave Mum this most . . . odd sort of look, almost as if he . . . rather liked her really. And she seemed to look at him in the same way. And, you know, when I took a good, close look at him myself, I saw that he wasn't old at all, not a bit. He was quite young, really – about Mum's age – and he had a nice smile and the most amazing, sparkling blue eyes. It was the famous whiskers that made him seem older, but then maybe he'd just grown them for the job. And when he said *'modom'* the way he did, I realised that there was quite a bit of fun in him and maybe a spot of mischief too. And I understood then that when he held the door open for all these rich people, the ones with the chauffeur-driven cars which waited for them parked out on the double yellow lines, that he was maybe making fun of them a bit, and he didn't really think that they were true 'modoms' at all.

But he seemed to think Mum was. Even if she wasn't rich and didn't have a load of money, he held the door open for her as if he thought she was a real lady. And despite everything he'd said to us before, calling us 'You lot!' and getting mad with us and not making us welcome – well, maybe he'd only been doing his job there too. Maybe he'd thought that we were just troublemakers and shoplifters. But now he could see we weren't. He could see that we were just ordinary and we didn't mean anyone any harm; we just had a few troubles, that was all.

I almost told him all about us living in the shop. But I didn't. That wouldn't have been fair. Because he did work there, after all. It wouldn't have been fair on him. He would have had something called torn loyalties then (at least I think that's what they're called). And he wouldn't have quite known what to do, whether to report us or not. And that would have put him on the horns of a dilemma – though I'm not quite sure what a dilemma is, but I think it might be a sort of cow. And another way of saying that kind of thing is to say that somebody is in a quandary. I'm not certain what a quandary is either, but you'd be sure to get one in Scottley's as they sell everything there.

'Thank you,' Mum said, as he held the door open for her. 'Thank you. That was very kind.'

'Not at all,' Mr Whiskers said. 'And what's the young lady's name?' he asked, ruffling little Angeline's hair.

'Geroff!' she said.

'Geroff?' he said. 'That's a nice name.'

'My name's not Geroff. My name's Angeline.'

'Well, that's almost as nice as Geroff. Maybe even nicer. And this young lady?'

'Livvy,' I said. 'Short for Olivia.'

'That's nice too,' he told me. And then Mr Whiskers looked at Mum and said, 'And what about *this* young lady?'

And did she *blush*! *Did* she! I thought she'd blushed back there in the cafeteria. But nothing like this. Talk about cherries. Talk about postboxes and tomato ketchup. She went absolutely crimson and she got all awkward and tongue-tied too. I'd never ever seen her like that. Usually Mum had an answer for everything. Even compliments.

'Geraldine,' she said. And then she recovered her composure. 'And what about this young man?' she said.

'Me? Martin,' Mr Whiskers said. 'That's my name.'

'Martin,' Angeline echoed. 'Martin Whiskers.'

And we all laughed. Not because it was that funny. More out of embarrassment and awkwardness than anything.

Some people came along then and Martin had to hold the door open for them.

'Morning, sir. Morning, modom,' he said, back to his old self. He let them in and once they were inside he turned and called after us.

'See you again, ladies.'

And we all giggled at him calling us ladies – even Mum – and it made you feel all warm and little and that you didn't have to worry about anything.

I began to quite like him then, which was funny, as I'd hated him before.

You can be so wrong about people, can't you? You can make such dreadful mistakes. It only goes to show, really, you shouldn't judge a person by his whiskers.

We went on down the road. I saw by the clock in Scottley's window display that the time was five past ten.

Five past ten. And we couldn't really go back until quarter to six. Almost eight hours; eight long hours to fill.

It was one of the longest days of my life.

'Where're we going to go, Mum?' little Angeline asked, after we had walked for a while.

'I don't know,' she said. Then she brightened up. 'Come on, let's go for a stroll in the park.'

So we went to the park and played on the swings and slides and climbing frames, and we looked at the ducks. We couldn't feed them as we didn't have any bread.

'I wish we'd brought some sell-bys,' Angeline said. 'Do ducks eat sell-bys?'

'No,' I said, 'only us. We're the sell-by family.'

But Mum just ignored me.

'Never mind, Angeline,' she said. 'The ducks don't look too hungry.'

It started to rain then – a slow, steady drizzle, the kind that seeps into your clothes and soaks you right through. We took refuge in the park shelter and watched the rain.

'What now, Mum? What can we do?'

'I know,' Mum said, 'the museum.'

So we went to the museum – but we couldn't go in. Because although it was free for me and Angeline, Mum had to pay for herself; and she didn't have enough money and they wouldn't let us in without her. I asked the man if he couldn't make an exception and let Mum in for nothing, but he said if he did it for her he'd have to do it for everyone (even though we were the only ones asking) and besides, he was only doing his job.

Why is it that you're never allowed to be kind to people when you're only doing your job?

So we went and sat in the Galleries instead, the indoor shopping centre, where at least it was dry. There was a man there playing a harp and trying to sell cassette tapes of his playing. We listened to him for a while. I wanted to give him some money, but Mum said we couldn't spare any just then, as we needed what we had for lunch.

The morning dragged by. Angeline got fractious and miserable and began to snuffle and said she wasn't well and was starting a cold.

'Let's go home, Mum. Let's go home to Scottley's and find a beanbag to lie on.'

Mum tried to explain to her that Scottley's wasn't really our home and didn't really belong to us, but it didn't do much good.

'I'm cold, I'm wet, I'm miserable, I'm hungry enough to eat a whole sell-by on my own and I want to go home!' little Angeline wailed.

And she spoke for us all. Mum and I felt the same; we were just too grown up to admit it. It seems to me that you're not allowed to be miserable once you're past a certain age. Your job then is to grin and bear it, and to pretend that everything's fine even when it stinks, and to say that it could all be worse – especially when it could be a whole lot better, and to say that there are millions of people worse off than you even when most of them aren't.

Mum bought us a bag of chips each and we stood and ate them in a shop doorway, but they were soon gone. It was one o'clock and there were still almost five hours to go before we could settle down in Scottley's for the night. It was so miserable, that long Saturday with no money to spend and nothing to do. I felt really sorry for the people who had no homes at all, the ones who slept out in cardboard boxes and blankets and who begged by the side of the road. It seems you can't do much without money, not on a cold, wet, miserable Saturday afternoon; you can't even go to the cinema. I did, I felt really sorry for all those people who sat begging in the underpass and I thought that, well, at least Mum and Angeline and I had a home to go to at the end of the day.

Only, did we? Did we really? And when I thought again, I realised with a sense of shock that we didn't. We were homeless too. We had no real home either. Just Scottley's. And what right did we have to be there? Nobody had invited us, or given us permission to stay there; we'd just helped ourselves, landed ourselves upon the place like uninvited guests. Not that we were doing any harm. We just had no right to be there, that was all. We had no key to the door, and a home's hardly a home when you haven't got the key to the door.

So yes, we were homeless too in our way. And what if, for some awful reason, we couldn't get back into Scottley's one night? Where would we go then? What would become of us? Would we end up huddled together in a shop doorway? Would we also have to live in a cardboard box

243

with the bitter cold seeping into us and the biting wind gnawing at our bones?

I began to get worried all over again, just like my old self. I hadn't been worried for hours and I hadn't even missed it. But now I was more worried and more afraid than ever, and the grey gloom of the day made it worse. Why did I have to be the worrier? How could Mum and little Angeline be so carefree so much of the time? Why did I have to be the responsible one in the family? Why did feeling responsible make you so unhappy?

'Where can we go, Mum? Where can we go?'

Little Angeline wasn't so carefree just then.

'I know,' Mum said, 'the library.'

So we went to the library and it saved our lives. It was warm and light and there was a special section for children, with thousands of books to read. There were low child-sized tables and chairs, and beanbags shaped like tortoises which you could sprawl out on while you read.

Mum left us there while she went to the adult section to get a book for herself. I found loads of picture books for Angeline so that she'd leave me in peace for a while to read what I wanted to on my own. And she did. She lay on her stuffed tortoise beside another girl and she looked at all the pictures and turned the pages, going 'Aw!' and 'Cor!' and 'Look at that!' and nudging the other girl to do so.

We stayed there until five o'clock when the library closed. We wanted to take some books out, but first we had to get tickets. In order to do that we first had to give the lady our address. But Mum didn't say it was Scottley's, she just said it was twenty-three the High Street and she'd bring a letter in to prove it tomorrow – and it was. Twenty-three the High Street just also happens to be Scottley's number. But who was likely to know that? Plainly not the librarian, who just gave a nod and handed our new tickets over, and there we were.

'Hurry along now,' Mum said, once we were back outside in the unwelcoming cold and damp. 'No dawdling. We need to get back in plenty of time so that we can hide up until the shop empties.'

So we hurried along the glistening streets. Darkness was coming down over everything and the street lights were going on. The shop fronts glowed warm and bright, and it made you think of fireplaces and hot cocoa, and snakes and ladders and jigsaws and things like that.

When we got near Scottley's, I looked up at Mum and said, 'Mum, do you think we'll see Mr Whiskers?'

And I think I must have sounded a bit hopeful and I was. In the past I used to dread seeing him, but now I was really quite looking forward to it. I wanted to check that I had been right about him and that he really was young behind the big whiskers, with blue eyes and a nice smile, and that I hadn't imagined it all.

'Maybe,' Mum said casually, 'maybe we'll see him,' and she shrugged.

But I think she was as hopeful as me and we headed for the side door at the east wing, where he had been in the morning.

We didn't see him though. I knew we wouldn't. You never do. That's the way things work. Something's always there when you don't want it, as soon as you do want it, it disappears. I don't know why it's like that, it just is. That was how they arranged the furniture when they made the world.

So we went inside and followed our usual routine. We walked around a while, waited until the coast was clear, then we slipped into customer ladies' and hid in one of the cubicles.

You'd think they'd have checked inside the cubicles before they locked the store, but they never did. We'd sometimes hear someone poking their head round the main door and mutter 'no one in here, fine,' but they never checked beyond that.

So there we were, in a cubicle again in customer ladies', all huddled together on the toilet seat, keeping our feet up so that no one could see them from under the door on the other side. We must have looked pretty comical, I know, but there was nothing funny in it for us. I'm sure we did look ridiculous, but it was just part of our lives now, hiding in a cubicle in customer ladies'; it was just what you did, part of the daily routine, like eating dinner and brushing your teeth.

At last the store emptied. The tills stopped ringing. Finally the doors were closed. We heard the staff call 'good night' to each other. 'Have a good weekend,' they said, just as they had a week ago, when we'd hidden under the big four-poster bed in Beds and Bedding.

A week ago? Was that all? It seemed an eternity. And there was still another three weeks to get through before we could move out to Western Drive. Or that was what I thought. I didn't for a moment think that this would be our last night, our very last night in Scottley's; that this was going to be the night when everything went haywire, the night when it all went finally and totally wrong.

CHAPTER SIXTEEN

Almost as if she'd had a premonition that everything was about to go bananas, Angeline made a last and most unusual request (the way people in stories do, when they're about to be shot the next morning and they want their favourite breakfast).

We were down in the Food Hall looking for sell-bys and Mum had just discovered a large, family-sized pizza that was in desperate need of eating before it went off.

'Pizza?' she suggested, and we both agreed.

'Okay. Pizza it is. And what shall it be for pudding?'

She began to look through the yoghurt tubs searching for one past its sell-by date, when Angeline made her unexpected request.

'Mum,' she said. 'Can we have ice cream?

'I don't think we'll find ice cream past its sell-by

date, Angeline. All the ice cream is frozen.'

'No, I mean pay-for-it ice cream. An ice cream sundae. Up in Ice Cream Heaven, Scottley's ice cream parlour.'

Mum looked rather shocked. And so did I.

'Ice Cream Heaven, Angeline,' she said. 'Scottley's ice cream parlour? Up on the fourth floor?'

'Yes.'

'But have you *seen* the ice creams there?'

'Seen the pictures.'

And that was true, we'd gone and drooled over them many a time, Angeline and I. We'd talked over which was the best ice cream sundae and which was the biggest and which would taste the nicest and which would take longest to eat. We'd even wondered how sick you'd feel after eating them. They were that enormous, with cream on them and sprinkles and chopped nuts and chocolate flakes and whole shortbread biscuits stuck in them sometimes, with toffee sauce poured all over and a little paper umbrella stuck in the top. (Not that you ate the little paper umbrella; you kept that for a souvenir or to pick your teeth with after, to stop them rotting away.)

'But Angeline,' Mum said, 'have you seen the

prices? They're so expensive. You could buy a whole meal for all of us for the cost of just *one* ice cream sundae up in Scottley's ice cream parlour.'

But money and the cost of things didn't really mean very much to little Angeline.

'That's all right,' she said, 'I don't mind.'

'Maybe not,' Mum replied, 'but I do.'

'Please, Mum,' Angeline said. 'We haven't had a treat for ages.'

'You're living in Scottley's,' Mum said, 'the best department store in town. Every day's a treat. Treats don't come much better than that.'

'Not an eating treat,' Angeline said. 'We haven't had an eating treat.'

And to be honest, I had to agree with her.

'She has got a point, Mum,' I said. 'We have been roughing it.'

'Roughing it?' Mum said. 'What do you mean, *roughing it*? This is luxury here in Scottley's, not roughing it!'

'Yes, maybe,' I said. 'But we have been living in a tent.'

And at least that got a smile out of her, if nothing else.

'We'll see,' Mum said. 'Come on, let's go and warm our sell-by up in *Staff Only*.'

So off we went with our pizza to put it in the *Staff Only* oven. But we knew we'd persuaded her. We did. We just knew it somehow, we had that feeling. And me and little Angeline kept looking at each other and grinning with excitement at the thought of those ice cream sundaes just waiting for us up in Scottley's Ice Cream Heaven and Delicious American Thick Milkshake Saloon (to give it its full title).

When the pizza was hot, we sat at our table in the staff canteen (funnily enough it was always the same table we chose too, although we had the choice of a hundred) and we ate our pizza slices and drank some sell-by milk and, you know, it was almost like a celebration, almost like a party.

Almost like a farewell.

Yes, I think that's what it was really. Not that we realised it at the time. Or maybe we did. Maybe we had the feeling that somehow this was going to be our last night in Scottley's and this was our way of saying thank you and goodbye, by having our little party there in the Staff Canteen. Yes, now I look back on it, I think I knew that something was going to happen; something big and tremendous and exciting, and that things would never be the same again. I think I felt that. I really did.

'Well, Mum?' little Angeline said, when the pizza was half-finished. 'Have you thought about our ice cream sundaes yet?'

'Well,' Mum said, 'how are they going to be paid for? That's the thing.'

'We'll do more cleaning and tidying, Mum,' we both said. 'Tomorrow.'

'We'll have to do an awful lot of cleaning and tidying to pay for three ice cream sundaes.'

'Just make it two then, Mum,' Angeline said. 'You don't have to have one.'

I don't think she meant to sound rude, she just thought she was making helpful suggestions.

'I don't want to just sit there and watch you two eating them! Huh!' Mum said. 'What a cheek!'

'I'll give you a spoonful,' little Angeline offered.

'If you're having one, I want my own one too!' Mum said. 'If I don't get one, nobody does.'

'Okay, Mum,' Angeline said kindly. 'You can have one then.'

'All right,' Mum said, 'but listen you two, tomorrow we do three hours cleaning and dusting to pay for them. Three hours each, right? And no moaning or changing your minds when it comes to the hard work. If you don't want to do three hours, say so now. Because we're certainly not stealing anything from Scottley's or taking what isn't ours, not even a spoonful of ice cream. Sell-bys are different, they'd only be thrown out anyway; but everything else has to be paid for one way or another. So are you prepared to do three hours' cleaning for an ice cream sundae or not?'

'We'll do it, we'll do it!' we chorused.

'We'll do three days' cleaning if you like,' Angeline offered.

'No, we won't,' I said, feeling that was too much, 'three hours is enough.'

'Three hours it is then,' Mum said. 'And remember – you promised. And what's more, you promised to do it without moaning.'

'Okay,' we said, and I was about to offer to cross my heart and hope to die and to spit on my hand as well, but I didn't think Mum would appreciate us spitting on our hands in the canteen, so I didn't mention it.

'All right. So come on then,' Mum said. 'Let's wash-up here and tidy away and then we'll head for Ice Cream Heaven.'

We washed and tidied and put off the staff canteen lights and up we went to the ice cream parlour. It was quite a large area, with seats for maybe sixty people, and it was all done out in pastel shades and pale ice cream colours, with cool white tiles on the floor. The tables were shaped like flattened-out ice cream cones and the chairs were like they were made out of wafers.

'Well, ladies,' Mum said, pretending to be a waitress, 'how many of you are there? A table for two, is it?'

'Yes,' Angeline said. 'Two will do.'

'Why not make it a table for three?' I suggested, 'and maybe you might like to join us?'

'Oh, how frightfully nice,' Mum said, in her posh waitress voice, 'I don't often sit down with the customers. But then I'm not often invited. So yes, I think I will. Ta, very much. A table for three it is then. Here we are, modoms, how about here by the window?'

'This will be ideal,' I said. 'We can look down at the city lights while we eat our ices. Just the thing.'

So Mum showed us to a window table and we sat down and then she picked up the menus and gave us one each.

'Would you care to see our selection?' she asked. 'Shall I give you time to make up your minds?'

'It's all right, thank you,' I said. 'I believe we already know what we want.' (And we did, because Angeline and I had spent quite some time in Ice Cream Heaven, looking at the menus and fantasising over what we might have.)

'Very well, modoms,' Mum said. 'Then shall I take your orders?' And she went and got an order pad and pencil from next to the desk and she licked the end of the pencil – the way proper waitresses sometimes do – to let us know she was ready and at our service.

'I,' I said, 'will have the Chocolate Cascade, please.'

Mum's eyes almost popped out.

'The Chocolate Cascade, modom? But does modom know what modom is taking on? A Chocolate Cascade? Will modom be able to finish it?'

'Modom thinks so,' I told her. 'Modom does.'

'Is modom sure that modom's eyes aren't bigger than modom's stomach?'

'Modom is quietly confident of success,' I said.

'But does modom know what is *in* a Chocolate Cascade? Does modom realise that a Chocolate Cascade consists of one dollop of chocolate-chip ice cream, one dollop of mint-choc-chip, one dollop of vanilla ice cream and one dollop of coffee-and-walnut, all served up with the largest jumbo-sized chocolate flake that modom has ever seen? And is modom also aware that the entire confection is placed in a huge glass and that grated chocolate is crumbled all over it, and that the whole thing is then smothered with whipped cream, and that chocolate and toffee sauce is then poured all over it, in alarmingly generous quantities, and then a wafer is struck in the top, just like a fairy on a Christmas tree? Is modom fully aware of this? Does modom know what modom is doing? Would modom not care to reconsider and maybe have a tiny, tiny helping of plain fat-free yoghurt instead?'

'No,' I said firmly. 'Modom would not. Modom has made her mind up and modom will stick to it. The Chocolate Cascade it is.'

'Very well, modom; as modom wishes.' Then Mum turned to little Angeline. 'And what will it be for smaller modom?' she said.

'Smaller modom,' little Angeline said, 'wants the same.'

The waitress nearly dropped her order pad.

'*The same*!' she shrieked. 'Smaller modom wants *the same* as bigger modom? A Chocolate Cascade too? With all the trimmings? Does smaller modom know what smaller modom is saying! Won't smaller modom be sick beyond imagining if smaller modom eats all that lot on top of pizza?'

'No!' smaller modom said most emphatically, 'smaller modom will *not.*'

'Oh my, oh my,' the waitress said. 'I can hardly believe my ears. But, well, the customer is always right, I suppose, so two Chocolate Cascades it is.'

And at that, we cheered.

'But what about you, Mum?' I said. 'That is – what about waitress modom? What is waitress modom going to have?'

'Waitress modom,' Mum said, her voice full of mischief, 'is going to have the same as well!'

'Hooray!' Angeline cried. 'We can all be ill together afterwards.'

'Hopefully it won't come to that,' waitress modom said. 'Now, if modoms would care to make themselves comfortable and look out of the window for five minutes, I will go and deal with your order.'

So off she went. We didn't sit and look out of the window though, we followed her over to the ice cream counter and watched as she prepared the three ice cream sundaes in three fluted glasses. By the time she'd finished, they looked just like the photographs in the menu.

'I'll carry them over,' she said. 'We don't want any accidents.'

So Mum put them on to a tray and over we went to our window seat, then Mum found spoons and napkins. Great long spoons they were too, so that you could get right down into the far corners of the glass to scrape out every last morsel of ice cream and chocolate. And then we began.

Now as soon as you started eating, you could tell why the place was called Ice Cream Heaven. Because it *was* heaven. It was the best. I've never had ice cream like it. It was so delicious. The chocolate was so chocolatey and the toffee was so toffee-ey, and it didn't make you feel sick at all. You just went on eating and eating, and each mouthful was even better than the last. And I tell you that if I ever die and if I get to go to heaven – well, the heaven I'll choose will be Scottley's Ice Cream Heaven, beyond a doubt. Because if that's not real heaven, well, it's definitely heaven on earth.

You should have seen us. By the time we'd finished eating, there was chocolate all over our faces. We had chocolate beards and chocolate moustaches – even Mum. I looked at her and said,

'Hey, Angeline, look who it is.'

'Who is it?' she said.

'Mrs Whiskers,' I said. 'Mrs Chocolate Whiskers.'

But she was too full-up to laugh.

We just sat there for ten minutes, looking at our stomachs and letting all the ice cream go down. Then Mum sighed and stood up.

'Anything else, modoms? she said.

'The same again, please,' Angeline said. But we knew she didn't mean it.

'Glass of water?' Mum said.

'Good idea.'

So we had some water to drink, then we took the dishes and spoons and washed everything up and put it all back where it belonged.

'Was it worth it?' Mum said. 'Was it worth the three hours' cleaning we're going to have to do?'

'It was worth three months' cleaning!' we said.

And it was.

We left Ice Cream Heaven and went down to retrieve our suitcase from the broom cupboard in customer ladies'. Then we went and washed and had showers, brushed our teeth and changed into our pyjamas.

'I must do some clothes washing soon,' Mum said. 'But not now. I'll leave it till the morning.'

So off we went to our tent down in Sports, Outdoors and Camping. It was still there. I wondered about the family we'd given such a fright to that morning when we'd suddenly appeared, as if from nowhere. I wondered if they'd bought one of the tents like ours. I hoped they had. It was a very good tent. I'd recommend it to anyone.

We got into our sleeping bags, Angeline and me, feeling full and happy and no longer thinking it strange for us to be living in a shop. Mum settled down on a canvas chair outside the tent to read a few pages of the book she had borrowed from the library that afternoon. She read by the light of a hurricane lamp which she had next to her chair.

'Good night, Mum,' we called.

'Good night,' she said. 'Lazy day tomorrow. Busy day at first, doing all the cleaning, then a lazy day after. We won't be able to go out though, I'm afraid. It'll be like last Sunday. But we can go back up on to the roof garden if the weather's fine.'

'That's okay,' I said, 'I don't mind staying in. I don't mind staying at home.'

And I fell asleep, dreaming of a lazy Sunday; imagining myself lying on the carpet in TVs and Stereos, watching the children's programmes on thirty televisions all at once.

And that should have been it until morning. But it wasn't. Because when I awoke it was still the middle of the night. And I knew that there was somebody else inside the store and that this time it wasn't the night watchman. Oh no, this time it was somebody else. I felt sick to my stomach. But it wasn't because of the Chocolate Cascade ice cream sundae, it was fear.

You see, I had the most awful feeling that there was something very strange going on, just above our heads. Just upstairs in the Jewellery and Precious Stones Department. Yes, something very strange indeed going on.

Something like a robbery.

CHAPTER SEVENTEEN

'Mum!' I called softly.

But she didn't wake up, so I prodded her again.
'Mum!'

She opened her eyes, stretched and went,
'Aaaah!' like she always did.

'What?'

'Listen!'

I could just make her out in the gloom of the
tent.

'What is it?'

'Someone moving about.'

'The security patrol?'

'No. He comes by between twelve thirty and
one. It's quarter to three now.'

I held up the clock with its luminous face (on
special offer from Clocks and Watches for a limited
period only) so that she could see the time.

'Maybe he's late?'

'But there's voices.'

'He's talking into his radio.'

'It's someone else, Mum, I'm sure. There's somebody else in the shop.'

Mum sighed a great tired sigh, the way she did when little Angeline woke her sometimes saying she needed the toilet or a glass of water or both.

'Don't you think we ought to investigate?'

'Oh, Livvy, are you *sure* you heard something?'

'Positive. Listen. *There*!'

A sound came from above us, as if somebody was up there using a drill.

'Maybe it's workmen,' Mum said.

'In the middle of the night?'

'Of course. When else would they work? The shop's empty then – or it's supposed to be. No customers in the way. It's an ideal time to do repairs and maintenance.'

The drilling stopped. There was silence, broken now and then by little Angeline gurgling in her sleep.

'Shall I go up and see, Mum?'

'No.'

'I'll only look. I won't do anything. I'll come straight back. And someone's got to stay with Angeline, haven't they? We can't just leave her here on her own. It's probably better if I go. I'm smaller and harder to see. I can duck down into the shadows.'

'No, Livvy!'

'Please! I'll come right back.'

'You won't do anything? Just look?'

'Promise.'

'And you'll come straight back?'

'Promise too.'

'Go on then. And Livvy—'

'Yes?'

'Borrow a torch from over there – on the display. But be careful with it. Don't let anyone see the beam.'

'Okay.'

'Five minutes only then. Or I'll wake up Angel and we'll come looking for you.'

'Five minutes. I heard.'

And I was on my way.

I crawled out from under the tent flap and kept on crawling over the floor of Sports, Outdoors and Camping until I found a torch. I didn't want to risk standing and then tripping over something in the half-light and making a noise.

I turned the torch on and made my way to the escalator, then I tiptoed up to the ground floor.

Once there, I put the torch off. I didn't need it as there was enough light in the ground floor department coming in from the street.

The drilling noise had started again and I headed in its direction. I padded silently and swiftly through the Food Hall, the tiled floor feeling cold under my feet. On I went past Ties and Handkerchiefs, along by the Gifts Department and deeper into the store.

The drilling grew louder still. I heard voices now, speaking in low tones – trying almost to whisper even – but the sound carried just the same, echoing through the empty departments.

I passed by Headscarves, I crossed the corridor that led to Umbrellas. I could smell that I was getting near to Soaps, Bath Salts and Shower Gels, and then the familiar scent of Perfumes and Aftershaves was in my nostrils. And there, just beyond Perfumes lay Jewellery and Precious Stones.

That was when I saw them: three shadowy figures. And it was all too plain what they were doing. They were breaking into the Jewellery Department and taking everything they could get their hands on.

I gasped.

One of them must have heard me.

I dropped like a stone down behind a counter display of Miss Modern Girl, a new perfume which the store was promoting that week.

'What was that?' a man's voice said.

'Thought I heard something too,' said a second.

'No, it's nothing,' another man told them. 'You're just getting jumpy. Come on, back to work.'

I waited a few minutes before daring to raise my head again. I hoped that Mum wasn't counting my five minutes too closely, because if she came looking for me with little Angeline in tow, and these three men saw her . . .

What if they had guns?

I watched, trying to make out what they were doing.

Jewellery and Precious Stones wasn't just an ordinary department in Scottley's. It had its own metal grille which was pulled down at night and locked to bolts set in concrete in the floor. It also had its own alarm system and we had been careful never to risk bumping into the grille for fear of setting the alarm off.

Each night the gems and jewels were cleared from their display cases and locked away behind the grille. The really expensive necklaces, rings and bracelets – the ones with the diamonds set in gold – were actually put away inside a safe. Some of those jewels were worth thousands and thousands of pounds too, which was why they were locked up.

Somehow the burglars had got round the grille alarm system and had drilled through the bolts securing the grille to the floor. I saw that two of them were putting gems and necklaces away into black holdalls, while the third man was turning his attention to the safe.

And then I gasped again. Or I think I did. Maybe I only thought a gasp. But I had to duck down behind the counter to try and calm myself, because my heart was beating nineteen to the dozen.

One of the burglars – I *recognised* him. There was no mistaking him, not even in the half light, not even at that distance.

And you know who it was? Yes, it was Mr Mysterious. It was Mr Mysterious himself. And then I understood why I'd kept seeing him and why he was always hanging around in Scottley's, looking here and there and getting the lie of the land and the feel of the place. No, he wasn't a store detective at all. He was a store robber.

But then, I thought, how did they get in? How did they break in without setting off the burglar alarms? Because there was only one door to the outside which didn't have an alarm to it in the whole building. Only one – the door to the roof garden. And that was it. That was what they must have done. Somehow they had got on to the roof of Scottley's and had come in down through the store. And now they had stolen half the jewels in the Jewellery Department and as soon as they got the safe open, they would steal the rest. Then they would escape the way they had come and nobody would be any the wiser – apart from us. We were the only ones who knew. We were the only ones who could stop them. Me and little Angeline and Mum.

I turned and scurried as quickly and silently as I could back down to the basement. In my hurry, I dropped the torch down the escalator and it clattered all the way to the bottom. But I don't think they heard, as the drilling went on without a pause. I found the torch, turned it on and hurried on through Sports, Outdoors and Camping to our tent. There was Mum, wide awake, waiting for me.

'Livvy! I was just about to come and look for

you. You've been nearly ten minutes.'

'I know, Mum. I know. I'm sorry, but I couldn't get back straightaway. Mum, there're *burglars* up there. Up on the ground floor. Up in Jewellery and Precious Stones, next to the Perfumery Department. Only it's not the perfumes they're stealing.'

'What?' Mum said. 'Burglars! How many?'

'Three. And guess who one of them is.'

'Who?'

'Mr Mysterious?'

'Mr *Who*?'

'In the cafeteria this morning – or rather yesterday morning now. The man I asked you about. I asked you if you thought he was handsome and you said yes maybe, but not as far as you were concerned.'

'Him!' Mum gasped. 'I knew there was something funny about him.' (I bet she hadn't though. She probably hadn't given him a second thought. She was probably only saying that now because it made her sound clever and like she'd known the burglary was going to happen and had suspected it all along.)

'They're drilling into the safe, Mum,' I said. 'What're we going to do to stop them?'

'But how did they get in' Mum said, 'without the alarms going off? Because as soon as you open the doors—'

'They must have come in from the roof,' I said. 'I've already worked it out.'

'But how did they get up on to the roof in the first place, Livvy? They don't have wings, do they?'

'Well, either they climbed up or climbed across from another building; or they were hiding up there all along, waiting for darkness and the store to close. Or maybe they even hid in a cubicle in customer gents'. Or perhaps they've got a helicopter.'

'A helicopter! Livvy, you can't just land a helicopter on the roof of Scottley's department store and expect people not to notice.'

'Well, maybe not then. But they must have some kind of plan for getting away. Mum, what are we going to do?'

'You wait here,' she said. 'First I need to see this for myself. Give me the torch a minute. You stay here in case Angeline wakes up. I won't be long.'

And before I could raise any objections, she was off.

She seemed to be gone ages and I started to get

really worried. I imagined that the burglars had seen her and had taken her prisoner and had tied her up with elastic rope from Car and Motoring Accessories, and had then put thick sticky tape over her mouth from Office and Stationery to stop her crying for help, and had put a big paper-clip over her nose as well, just to be nasty. Or maybe they'd locked her in a trunk from Luggage and Cases and had covered it over with some rugs from Rugs, Mats and Floor Coverings so as to muffle the thumps.

But no, she was all right. After about fifteen minutes I saw a torch light come down the escalator and move towards our tent.

'Livvy?' Mum whispered.

'Here, Mum!'

'You all right? Angeline okay?'

'Fine. Still asleep. Did you see them?'

'Yes.'

'Have they got into the safe yet?'

'No, but they've stopped drilling. I think they're going to put some explosive in now to try and blow the door open.'

'No! Mum, *What* shall we *do*? We'll have to get the police.'

'But Livvy, if we get the police and they find us

here as well as the burglars, what are they going to think? What will they make of that?'

Of course I hadn't even stopped to consider that aspect of it. Because what were we doing in Scottley's after all? We had no right to be there either. In fact we were burglars too, in a way. We hadn't exactly broken in and we hadn't exactly stolen anything (because you couldn't count eating old sell-bys as stealing) but how would the police see it? They'd only see us as being intruders too and we'd get arrested along with the real thieves. Maybe they'd even think that we were all part of the same gang – though I must admit that little Angeline was a bit young to be a desperate criminal.

So what to do?

'Perhaps we can get the police and then hide until they've arrested the burglars, Mum? Hide until they've arrested them and gone.'

'I don't think so, Livvy. Once the police come, there's going to be people all over the place. They're going to look everywhere; they're bound to find us.'

'Then maybe we should just go back to sleep then, Mum, and let them get on with stealing the jewels and just pretend it's not happening.'

'Livvy!' Mum said. 'I'm surprised at you!'

'Well, maybe you are, Mum,' I said, 'but I get fed-up with being good and sensible and responsible all the time. I get really cheesed off with it sometimes and that's the truth. I'm fed-up always trying to do the right thing. I never get any thanks for it.'

'Maybe, Livvy, but how would you like it if somebody just stood by and let *your* belongings get stolen.'

'I haven't got any belongings worth stealing, Mum,' I pointed out. 'In fact I've hardly got any belongings at all. And I can't see I'm likely to ever have any, not the way things are going. And while I do know that money isn't everything, Mum, and toys and possessions aren't everything either, it might be nice to have something that was mine, even if it was only little.'

Mum pretended she hadn't heard half of what I'd said. Maybe she felt a bit guilty about it because she knew it was true, and I'd maybe hurt her feelings. But that's the trouble with hitting the nail on the head, you usually bang someone on the thumb while you're doing it, or hammer it into them by mistake.

'Well, just say you *did* have a lot of things then,'

Mum argued. 'Or even a few things. You wouldn't want them stolen, would you?'

'Suppose not.'

'Then we can't just go back to sleep, can we? And if we can't call the police because we'll get into trouble too, then we'll just have to stop the burglars ourselves.'

'*Us?*' I said. 'You and me and little Angeline? How are we going to stop three desperate criminals with drills and bolt-cutters and plastic explosive? Mum, be reasonable!'

'I've got an idea,' Mum said. 'Let's see how they're planning to get away. Come on. Up on to the roof.'

'But Mum, what about Angeline? We can't just leave her here gurgling. What if the burglars hear her? They might pinch her too and hold her to ransom or something.'

'We'll take her with us, of course. Come on.'

With that, Mum gathered Angeline up in her arms and carried her towards the escalator. Angeline gurgled a bit at being moved suddenly, but she didn't waken.

'Come on, Livvy,' Mum said, 'and bring the torch. Let's go. Up to the roof.'

CHAPTER EIGHTEEN

Well, it practically killed me walking all the way up to the roof of Scottley's when I was totally exhausted to start with and had only had a few hours' sleep. It was a strain keeping quiet too. I was afraid that the slightest sound might be heard by the burglars and that they'd realise they weren't alone and come after us.

But we got up to the top floor without incident. Mum pushed the door to the roof garden open and we went out into the chill of the night. Angeline shivered and began to wake.

'Cold,' she said. 'Bad dream.'

'Won't be long, Angel,' Mum comforted her. 'Just be out here a minute.'

We had a look around. There was plenty of light. The moon was almost full and the sky was clear and the glow of the city rose up to meet us.

'Look,' Mum said. 'Here.'

She'd found some rucksacks. She gave me Angeline to hold, opened the rucksacks and took out what was in there. There were coils and coils of rope. Miles and miles of it. And there were metal spikes and metal loops and all the things that you use in rock climbing, which I recognised immediately from having spent so much time in Sports, Outdoors and Camping.

'You were right, Livvy,' Mum said. 'They must have hidden up here when the shop closed, waited until the night security patrol had been and gone, and then down they went into the store – through the only door that isn't alarmed. And once they've got what they came for, they're going to abseil down over the side of the building, all the way down to the ground.'

'What's abseil mean, Mum?'

'Basically, to slide down on a rope.'

'Cor!'

'Look!'

Mum was staring down over the parapet into the alleyway far below. There was an expensive-looking car parked down there, half-hidden in the shadows.

'Must be their car,' Mum said. 'For the getaway.'

Well, my head was spinning looking down at

that car, it was so far away. And I tell you, they might have been burglars those three men, but they must have been brave ones. Because there was no way that I would slide down on a rope from the roof of Scottley's department store all the way to the ground. Not unless I had about thirty parachutes and a hot-air balloon and about twenty-five soft mattresses to land on if I fell.

'So what do we do, Mum?'

'I know,' she said. 'We do this.'

And she went and got the coils and coils of rope, and you know what she did?

That's right. She threw them over the parapet, down into the alleyway below. One rope uncoiled as it fell and landed with a clatter on the roof of the car.

'Right,' Mum said. 'That's put paid to their escape route. They're cornered now. Their only way out is through one of the doors. And as soon as they open that, the alarms will go off.'

And she dusted her hands and seemed rather pleased with herself.

'But Mum,' I said. 'If *they're* cornered, so are *we*. When they come up here and find their ropes missing, they're going to know that someone else is—'

Then I stopped in mid-sentence as a faint, muffled noise came from far away underneath us. It was a kind of *kerummph*! sound followed by a dull thud.

'Cold,' Angeline said. 'Want to go inside.'

'The safe,' I said. 'They've done it. They've blown the door off.'

'Yes,' Mum said. 'Now they'll grab what's in there and any minute—'

'They'll be up here!' I said. 'And they'll find us. And when they see that you've thrown their ropes off the roof, they'll probably throw us off after them.'

'Don't be silly, Livvy, of course they won't,' Mum said. But she didn't sound too confident. 'We'd best get out of the way though, just the same. Come on. Let's hide.'

We went back inside and closed the roof door quietly behind us.

'Quick, hurry,' Mum whispered. 'Let's get away from these stairs.'

That flight of stairs was the only way down from the roof. If we'd met them there, we'd have been done for.

'Where to?'

'Anywhere. This way. Come on.'

Already we could hear voices and footsteps drawing nearer, rising up the stairwell. The burglars must have blown the safe open, taken its contents, and now were hurrying to get away as swiftly as possible.

'Here we are. In here.'

We ducked into the first department we came to up on the top floor: School Uniforms and Children's Shoes. It was filled with rows and racks of dark blazers and grey trousers and grey skirts and striped ties.

'Tired,' little Angeline muttered, as I carried her along. 'Want to go back to bed.'

'Mum,' I said, 'can you take her again? She's getting heavy.'

Mum took her from me and we moved on to the far end of the department.

'In here,' Mum said, and we went into one of the changing cubicles where you go to try your new school uniform on and we closed the door.

We sat on the floor. Mum cradled Angeline on her lap. And that was when I noticed it. One of her slippers had gone.

'Angeline! Where's your slipper?'

'Don't know. Want to go back to sleep.'

She shut her eyes. Mum and I stared at each other

'Where is it, Livvy? I put her slippers on her before we came up.'

'Both of them?'

'Yes.'

'It must have fallen off.'

'What if they see it?'

'Hold on. Maybe it's just outside. I'll go and look.'

'Careful.'

I poked my nose round the door of the changing cubicle like a mouse peeking out though a hole in the skirting. The coast was clear. I retraced our steps, looking for Angeline's slipper. It was nowhere to be seen. I went on, getting nearer to the stairwell. The voices were louder now. They could only be one flight away at the most.

'How much do you think?' one of the voices asked.

'Couple of hundred thousand at least,' the second voice answered. Then there was a third voice. I recognised it as belonging to Mr Mysterious.

'Come on, you two. Let's get away. We can count it up later.'

Then I saw their shadows growing larger upon the wall as they ascended the stairs.

I froze. I couldn't move. I just froze and stood there by the racks of Skirts, Grey Medium. I saw them coming up the stairs; I saw the outlines of their faces. One of them even looked straight at me, I'd swear he did. But he didn't see me. He just saw the clothes. Then they were gone, upwards and onwards to the roof. I heard their footsteps and then the rumble of the door to the roof garden being pushed open.

Any second now they would find that their ropes had gone. They might even see them lying far away down in the alley, one of them lying like a dead snake on the roof of their car. Then they would probably find something else too – Angeline's slipper. That must be where it was. Up there on the roof. That was where it must have fallen off her foot.

Yes, any second now they'd find the slipper.

And then what would they do?

I unfroze. My heart was thumping so hard it thumped me back to life. I ran back to where Mum and Angeline were hiding in the changing cubicle.

'Livvy, did you find it? Did you get her slipper?'

'No. It must be on the roof. And they're up there now. They'll see and they'll know, Mum. They'll know we're here. They'll come looking for us! Oh Mum!'

And there I was, worrying again.

Then there were voices. Loud, angry, maybe even rather frightened voices and there was the slamming of the roof door.

'I'm *sure* I left them there, *sure* I did!'

'Well, where are they now then?'

'How do I know?'

'So now what do we do?'

'Stop panicking. Use your head. Wait. There's a Sports Department. Where's that?'

'In the basement.'

'There'll be ropes there. Let's go and get them.'

'Wait up, what's this?'

'What?'

'Here on the stairs. What's this?'

'Kid's slipper, isn't it?'

'What's that doing there?'

'Forget about it. Some kid lost it. Come on.'

'No, wait. That wasn't here before.'

'What do you mean?'

'It wasn't here when we came down . . . There's someone else here . . . Someone in the building.'

Little Angeline let out a long, loud gurgle. Mum

283

tried to put her hand over her mouth, but it was too late. They'd heard us.

'What's that?'

'There is! Someone's there.'

'Okay. Let's get moving.' It was Mr Mysterious talking now; he seemed to be the one in charge. 'You go get the ropes from the basement, Don. Come on, Lee, you and I'll go and see who's there. And if there *is* anyone, we'll make sure they stay quiet.'

One set of footsteps hurried off down the stairs. The clatter of them faded away. Then I heard Mr Mysterious's voice again.

'You take that side. I'll look here.'

And I knew that he was coming towards us.

I could hear his footsteps; not even the thick pile of the carpet completely muffled them. Everything else was so quiet, the silence magnified every sound. It made the beat of your heart and the pumping of your blood sound like thunder to you. He'd hear us, surely he'd hear us. He must be able to hear my heart beating. You could probably hear it two miles away.

Nearer he came, nearer and nearer. You could hear the rattle of a coat-hanger as he bumped into one of the racks of clothes. Nearer and nearer, moving towards the changing area now, nearer and nearer still. I wanted to say something; I wanted to hear Mum's voice. But it was too dangerous. Our only hope was silence.

Nearer still. Just like Hide and Seek. Cold at first, then getting warm, then getting even warmer, then hot, then very hot.

There were five changing cubicles in a line. We were in the fourth from the left – the last but one.

Creeak!

He pushed open the door of the first cubicle and must have peered inside.

Hot. Very hot. Very hot and getting hotter.

The first cubicle door clattered shut. Another creak then as the second cubicle door was opened. Very, very hot now. Almost boiling. The second cubicle door swung shut. I could hear his breath. I could all but see him. He was there. He was right there.

Creeak!

Third cubicle door. Boiling now. So, so hot. Sun-beating down, desert hot. So boiling, blistering, scalding hot. And getting even warmer. Temperature still rising. Fahrenheit to centigrade. He was coming now. His hand was on the door. He wasn't just hot now, he was on fire. His mysterious hand was on fire. The door was on fire; it vanished, disappeared; there was no door. The door was open and there he was, looking at us. Mr Mysterious. And he didn't look handsome any more, he looked vicious and cruel and angry and evil and –

'So what have we here?' he said. 'Just what have we here? You three, is it? I see. I get it. I wondered why I kept seeing you three and now I know. You're living here, aren't you? Taken up residence. It was you, wasn't it, who threw our ropes off the side? Think that was a clever thing to do, do you? Well, let me tell you, ladies, you may have been living here up to now, but you won't be living here much longer. In fact, you won't be living *anywhere* much longer. You won't even be *living*. Come here!'

Then he reached out and just as he did, Mum yelled, 'Now, Livvy! Now! Run! *Run for your life!*' And she gave him the most tremendous kick in the shins (which my mum is rather good at actually, because she used to play ladies' football) and he doubled over yelling, 'Ow, ow, ow!' and several worse things as well, which I couldn't possibly repeat as children aren't supposed to know words like that and I wouldn't want to get anyone into trouble, especially myself.

Then we ran. But we didn't get far before he started limping after us. And soon he wasn't even limping. He was running too, despite the pain in his leg. He was after us and he was calling for the other man to come and help him.

And we were running. Running for our lives. Running like the devil himself was after us.

CHAPTER NINETEEN

Well, he might have been bigger than us and he might have been stronger and he might have been faster, but he didn't know Scottley's like we did. He only knew it in the daytime; we knew it in the dark.

We dashed from the cubicle and headed for the escalator.

'Lee! They're going down!' Mr Mysterious shouted, as he stumbled along behind us. 'Get after them. Head them off!'

We ran down the escalator and found ourselves in the Toy Department.

'This way, Mum,' I said, and I led the way, dashing along by the boxes of toys. It was like a maze there, a warren of shelves and displays and of nooks and crannies, and I was familiar with every one. I looked behind us once and I made out two figures chasing after us – one of them still limping slightly.

'Where to, Livvy?' Mum said, breathless from carrying little Angeline.

'This way!'

I made a sudden left turn and then there we were.

'In here, Mum!'

And I dashed inside the Wendy House.

Mum followed me inside and we crouched down low as the two men ran past. Little Angeline had actually gone back to sleep, cradled in Mum's arms.

'Where now? Where have they got to?' I heard Mr Mysterious say. 'And where's Don with those ropes?'

'He'll be on his way,' the man called Lee answered.

'He'll wonder where we are. He's expecting us to be up by the roof. You stay here. Keep an eye out for that woman and the brats. I'll go check he's all right.'

Footsteps again. Moving away this time. Mr Mysterious had gone, leaving the other man, Lee, somewhere nearby, standing guard in case we should reappear.

'We've got to ring for the police, Mum,' I

whispered. 'Even if we get into trouble as well. We have to now, don't we?'

'Yes,' she said. 'Yes, I know. Only how do we get to a phone?'

Then little Angeline suddenly opened her eyes wide, stared around her, muttered, 'Oh look, we're in the Wendy House,' and then she shut them tight again and went on gurgling as if she hadn't woken at all.

'I know, Mum,' I said. Computers and Telecommunications.'

'What about it?'

'It's full of mobile phones. One of them must be working.'

'Okay. Let's try and get there.'

Carefully we straightened up and peered out of the Wendy House window. We could just discern a distant figure standing guard at the end of the department, where the four aisles connected at a kind of crossroads – just where the Toy Department met up with Cushions and Chair Covers. There he was, standing by a great big heap of beanbags one piled on top of the other, reaching up like a mountain almost to the ceiling.

'We'll never get past him,' Mum said. 'He'll see us. Or hear us.'

'Yes,' I said. 'I know.' And it really did seem impossible.

But then I got it. I don't get many ideas, but when I do get them, they're good ones. And I reckon that this one was one of my best – though maybe that's not really for me to say and you'll have to make your minds up as to what you think of it for yourselves.

It was the cars.

Remember the cars? The toy cars I told you about? The ones that cost thousands of pounds? The ones that all the rich people buy for their sons and daughters to drive about on the private roads of their vast estates? Well, they were the ones. There they were, all parked in a line, with a sign on them reading *Do Not Touch. Please Ask An Assistant For Help If Needed*.

'Mum,' I whispered. 'Look. The cars. The little Range Rover.' And I pointed at the small, electrically-driven, scaled-down model of a Range Rover out on the floor of the Toy Department.

'What about it?'

'Show you when we get there. Come on.'

We crept out from the Wendy House and tiptoed towards the car.

'Can you drive, Mum?' I asked.

'Sort of,' she said, which I took to mean no but she'd have a try. When we got to the Range Rover though, she was too big to fit in the driving seat.

'I'll have to do it, Mum. You sit in the back with Angeline.'

She got into the back. Angeline woke up properly this time. She looked around wild-eyed but didn't say a word. She carried on as if it was all perfectly normal to be sitting in the back of a scaled-down, working model of a Range Rover in Scottley's Toy Department at half past three in the morning.

Finally she spoke.

'Where we going?' she whispered.

'For a little trip,' I told her, and my hand reached for the starter.

It hardly made a sound – little more than a computer being turned on. The electric motor purred quietly, barely noticeable above the hum of Scottley's air-conditioning and heating system, which was always on.

I pressed my foot on to the accelerator pedal and the small Range Rover glided away. It wobbled a bit at first, as I wasn't used to steering; but I soon had the hang of it. After all, I'd been on the dodgems once and Mum had let me drive, so I wasn't a complete beginner. I mean, I didn't need L-plates or anything.

Off we went along the aisle. There at the far end, standing at the crossroads, was the man, Lee; his back towards us, his hands by his sides, something heavy-looking in one of them – maybe a small truncheon that he carried with him (a cosh I think they're called) or maybe it was even a gun.

For a moment I thought of turning the Range Rover's lights on, but no, I decided that it would be too dangerous. He might see them reflected in one of the shop windows and turn around. I pressed my foot a little harder down on to the accelerator. The speedometer crept up from five . . . to seven . . . to ten . . . to twelve miles an hour.

'Seat belts on in the back!' I hissed at Mum and Angeline, and I heard the click of the belt buckles as they slid into their catches.

'Put on your own!' Mum whispered to me, and I did, just about managing to do it with one hand on the steering wheel and the other manipulating the belt.

'*Whee*!' Angeline said. 'We're getting a lift!'

'Shhh!' Mum told her, and on we sped down the aisle.

I pressed my foot right down flat to the floor. The speedometer needle crept up to fifteen miles per hour.

We zoomed on down the aisle. There the man was, just ahead of us. The electric engine of the Range Rover was getting louder now and the tyres were rumbling. Any second now he'd turn and see us. But not before I'd –

'Livvy!' I heard Mum hiss into my ear. 'What are you doing? You're not going to run into him! You'll kill him, for heaven's sake! What are you going to do?'

'Don't worry,' I said, 'it's all under control, I'm just . . .'

Then there we were, right behind him, no more than a couple of feet away. And that was when I did it. I reached forward and I leant on to the car horn with all my weight.

Paaaaaaarrrrrrrrrppppppp!

And you should have seen him! He spun round; he saw us; a look of total horror and disbelief came into his face, followed by an expression of complete and utter panic. He must have thought he was going bonkers. Because it's not really what you expect to see, is it? Not when you're burgling Scottley's department store and stealing all the jewellery in the middle of the night. The last thing you expect to come across is three people in their pyjamas and nighties sitting in a fully-working model Range Rover, driving down the aisle of the Toy Department straight at you at about fifteen miles an hour. Especially when they're blasting the horn at you and flapping their arms like mad things, yelling, 'Get out of the way or you'll be killed!' And especially when one of them is a little girl, who's sitting in the back seat waving at all the toys and dolls she passes as if she were the Queen, saying, 'How nice to see you. How very good of you all to come. A special hello to all you teddy bears. Too kind, too kind.'

For a split second he was rooted to the spot. At any moment we were going to flatten him. Then, as I'd hoped, he jumped out of the way. He made this tremendous dive – just as if he were a goalkeeper making an impossible save – and he went head first into the tower of cushions and beanbags.

Down they came. It was like a great skyscraper collapsing. Cushions and beanbags fell like rain. One landed on the bonnet of the Range Rover.

'Help!' I yelled. 'I can't see where we're going! I can't see a thing! We're going to crash!'

For a second or two I lost control. The Range Rover left the aisle and veered off towards Upholstery Materials and Soft Furnishings. I fought to get the beanbag off the bonnet, jerking the wheel to dislodge it.

'Left!' Mum screamed. 'Or it looks like curtains! Well, it's that or venetian blinds!'

I wrenched the wheel. Mercifully the beanbag fell off and I could see where I was going again. I got the Range Rover out of the rough and back on to the road (well, the aisle, anyway).

As we drove on, I glanced into the rear-view mirror to see what had become of the man back at the crossroads. He had disappeared under the great pile of beanbags, but I couldn't imagine that they'd have done him any harm. He'd probably tunnel his way out in a minute, but by that time we'd be gone.

'Where to now?' Mum said. 'Where are we going, Livvy?'

'Computers and Telecommunications, of course,' I said, 'to ring for the police.' And I pulled the wheel to the right – forgetting even to indicate, so it was a good job there wasn't anybody coming the other way – and we whizzed off through Wallpaper, Paints and Stencilling at twenty miles an hour (our top speed).

'You're going too fast, Livvy!' Mum shouted.

'*Wheee*!' little Angeline squeaked. 'I like this. *Wheee*! We're all going for a *wheee*!'

'Too fast, Livvy, too fast! Slow down!'

'We've got to get to a phone, Mum,' I yelled back. 'Before they get away.'

So on we sped, past the shelves of wallpaper and the pots of paint. The rows of brushes seemed to wave at us, urging us on. Then they were far behind us and we were rushing through the half-darkness, past Cameras and Photography, and Hair and Beauty, and then there we were, in Computers and Telecommunications. I stood on the brake and the Range Rover came to a halt. I turned off the engine and sat a moment to get my breath.

'Wow!' I said. 'Everyone all right?'

'I'll never be the same again,' Mum said. 'I'm practically a nervous wreck.'

'That was great,' little Angeline said. 'Bestest ever. Let's go and do it again – only backwards and wearing blindfolds.'

'Over my dead body,' Mum said, and she unclipped her seat belt. 'Come on, let's find a phone.'

Well that was easy enough. There were hundreds of them. But none of them worked. They were all either on display or stacked up in boxes, but none of the mobile phones seemed to be charged-up or connected.

'Come *on*,' Mum said, muttering to herself as she picked up yet another phone, put it to her ear, listened for a dialling tone that wasn't there, and then discarded it to try yet another. 'Come on. Come on, come on. Come on, before they find us.'

She seemed worried. And I was worried too. (Naturally.) I could hear the voices of the three men calling angrily to each other through the store. All efforts at whispering and all attempts to keep things quiet had gone.

'Lee! Where are you?' It was the voice of Mr Mysterious.

'Here! Under these beanbags! Help dig me out!'

'What're you doing there? It's no time to be lying down on a beanbag having a rest!'

'I'm not lying on them. I'm not having a rest! Those – (and he used a very rude swearword here, another of those ones which children aren't supposed to know; in fact even grown-ups aren't supposed to know it) '– kids ran me over in a car.'

'Ran you over? In a car? What're you talking about?'

'Come on, let's get after them.'

'Forget them. No time for it. Don's got the ropes. Come on. Back to the roof.'

Mum frantically went from one phone to the next, growing more and more agitated.

'No use!' she groaned. 'None of them working. Not one of them.'

'Come on, Mum,' I said. 'Try this one, try another.'

'Hello,' little Angeline said, talking into one of the dead phones, playing at making phone calls. 'Angeline here. Anyone there want to talk to me?'

Then I saw the phone on the wall.

'Mum! Scottley's phone. Use this one.' I put it to my ear and heard the buzzing of the dialling tone. 'It's working. It's on line.'

'It's just an internal phone though, isn't it?' Mum said. 'It's just for making calls to other departments within the store. We need an *outside* line.'

'Well, try it, anyway.'

'What do you need for an outside line . . .? Now, you normally have to dial nine first, isn't that it?'

She pressed the nine.

'Well? Well, Mum?'

'Yes,' she said. 'Got it! An outside line!'

'Well, go on then, Mum. Go on. Ring for the police. Go on, Mum. Dial nine-nine-nine. Quick. Before they get away.'

But she didn't. She put the phone back on to its cradle.

'What, Mum? What is it?' I all but screamed.

'Listen you two, before I ring – you've got to understand something. If I call the police – well, okay, they might catch the thieves, but they'll catch us too. Do you understand? They'll find us here and find out all about us living in Scottley's and about us sleeping in the Sports, Outdoors and Camping department and all the rest. And to be honest, we had no right to do it. And it was all my idea. It's all my fault we had to come here. It's because I'm not very good at organising things and I'm not very good with money sometimes either. And, you know, I do love you both, more than anything in the whole world. But the truth is . . . I'm not a very good mother.'

'Oh, you are, Mum, you are,' I said, and I grabbed her and I held her as tight as I could. 'You're the best mum there is. You are! Isn't she, Angeline?'

'Best mum ever,' Angeline said. 'Best one ever made. Best mum in the whole of Scottley's.' And as she wasn't tall enough to grab Mum round the waist, she grabbed her round the leg instead and she wouldn't let go.

'No, I'm not,' Mum said. 'I'm not. I'm irresponsible and stupid and I don't deserve to have you. I shouldn't have brought you here. It was just a stupid, reckless thing to do.'

And you know, maybe it was. I had to admit it. I knew it was. I can't help being sensible. I'd known it all along. But it was more than that too. And I had to say so.

'Mum,' I said, 'it might not have been the most responsible thing to do, bringing us to live in Scottley's, but I have to tell you, I'm glad we came. It's been the greatest adventure ever, hasn't it Angeline? The greatest adventure anyone could have had. And I'll remember it always, till I'm so old that I can hardly remember anything any more. But there's one thing I'll never forget: that I had a marvellous mum and she brought us to live in Scottley's. And while all the other children were sleeping in their bedrooms – same as they did every night, same as boring usual – *we* were sleeping in Scottley's. And while they only had their toys to play with, we had a whole Toy Department. And while they only had a small table to eat at, we had a whole staff canteen. And while they only had *one* TV to watch, we had *hundreds*. And while they only had toy cars to play with, we were riding round in a real, live, scaled-down Range Rover. And while other children only read about burglars and mysteries and having to be brave, we met *real* burglars and *real* mysteries and we really *did* have to be brave. And I'd rather have had that, Mum, than all the tea down in Scottley's Tea and Coffee Department. I really would. Because adventures are the best. Adventures are more than jewels and gems and precious stones. They're even better than worrying. Adventures are more than anything and people are better than things. And it doesn't matter if we don't have any money, Mum, because we've got you. And as long as we've got you, we'll always have adventures. And that's right, isn't it, Angeline? That's so, isn't it? That's truer than true.'

But little Angeline didn't say anything, she just nodded her head and then she offered Mum her tissue from the sleeve of her pyjamas, as Mum seemed to have something in her eye.

'Okay,' Mum said, after she'd blown her nose,

'but there's one more thing I've got to tell you, and I should have told you this long, long ago. It's about your dad. Your dad isn't working on the oil rigs in Arabia. I don't really know where he is any more. Your dad was a bit irresponsible too and he just sort of drifted away years ago – when you were still little, Livvy, just after Angeline was born. He did love you both; he just couldn't face up to his responsibilities. And to be honest, I don't think we'll ever see him again now. I'm sorry. I should have told you a long time ago. I know I should. I'm sorry I didn't. I was a coward. It was easier to pretend than to tell the truth.'

Angeline and I looked at each other. But we didn't cry or anything. You see, we may not have been grown-up, but we weren't stupid. I think we'd known all along that it was just a story, about Dad working in the oil rigs and how he was going to come back one day and we'd all be rich. We kind of knew he'd gone.

'It's all right, Mum.' I said, 'I think we already knew. Just as long as we've got each other, you and me and Angeline. Just as long as there's the three of us. That'll be fine. We'll manage. It'll be all right.'

Mum blew her nose on the tissue again and then

she straightened up and she looked more like her old self: proud and straight and determined, and with that gleam of mischief in her eye.

'Do I phone for the police then? And tell them about the burglars? What do you think?'

'Yes,' I said. 'Let's do the right thing, Mum. After all, we have to look after the place. We do live here.'

'Yes,' Angeline agreed. 'We do live here. It's our home.'

'Okay,' Mum said. 'We'll do the right thing.'

So she took up the telephone again, dialled nine for an outside line, and then dialled nine-nine-nine for the emergency services. I heard her ask for the police and then I heard her say, 'Hello, I wish to report a robbery . . . In Scottley's department store . . . Yes. That's correct . . . Right now . . . They're up on the roof. But you'd better be quick before they climb down. They've taken ropes from Sports, Outdoors and Camping . . . Yes . . . How do I know? Oh, simple – because I live here.'

CHAPTER TWENTY

Well, you know the rest for yourselves, I suppose. How the police cars all came, and how they caught Mr Mysterious and his two friends just as they abseiled down from the roof on the ropes they had taken from Sports, Outdoors and Camping. You must know too that the police recovered all the jewellery from the holdall that Mr Mysterious had clipped to his belt, and that the three men were arrested and taken off in a van.

Then, of course, the manager of Scottley's turned up with all his bunches of keys and everyone came into the store and they found us down in the basement, just finishing our packing and all changed into our day clothes, as Mum didn't want us to be found in our pyjamas.

The policemen said we had to go along with them and Mum said did we *have* to, but they said we did. But before she'd go, Mum was very particular to point out that everything was neat and tidy in the Sports, Outdoors and Camping and it was all just as we'd found it – wasn't that right? And Scottley's manager – who looked a bit bleary-eyed at being woken in the middle of the night – had to agree that the place was absolutely spotless and you'd never have known we'd been staying there at all and we'd kept it so clean you could have eaten your dinner off the carpet if you'd been that way inclined.

Then off we went in a police car and they brought us here first; but because it was so late, someone said that they couldn't possibly start asking us questions now, and so they found us all somewhere to sleep – me and Mum and Angeline together – and we slept for ages and had a good long lie-in. Then, in the morning, they brought us back here again and you've been asking us questions ever since. And to be honest, I'm just about fed-up with them and I've told you all I can and I've nothing more to say.

Oh, apart from one thing. And this is really important. When we were brought back to the police station this morning, there was someone waiting for us, waiting to ask if he could help us in any way.

Did you see him? Did you see him in the waiting room? Didn't you? Can you guess who it is? No? Well go and have a look. You can't miss him. And he says he won't go home until he knows what's going to happen to us. You do know who it is, don't you? Don't you? Really? Can't you imagine?

Well, it's Mr Whiskers, of course. Yes, that's right. He looks rather different out of his doorman's uniform, but you'd recognise his moustache anywhere.

So we're not alone, see. We do have someone; we do have a friend. So you'd better not think you can do anything with us or go trying to split us up, because we're not the only ones you'll have to contend with. There's Mr Whiskers too. And he knows lots of important people. He knows how to open doors, see. So you'd just better not try to split us up, that's all. Or there'll be trouble.

SERGEANT CLARKE:

Livvy, I can assure you that splitting your family up is the last thing we want to do.

MRS DOMINICS:

Each case does, however, have to be considered on its merits.

W.P.C. MATHLEY:

Oh, do stop being so pompous!

MY DIARY

THIS IS LIVVY'S PERSONAL PROPERTY. DO NOT TOUCH, DO NOT READ, DO NOT DARE OPEN THIS DIARY. THIS IS PRIVATE. READ THIS DIARY AND YOU ARE DEAD SEVERAL TIMES OVER, PROBABLY WITH KNOBS ON.

TUESDAY 7TH. THINGS ABOUT TODAY.

I haven't been keeping my diary every day, not like I promised way back in January when it was new and when I swore to write something for every day of the year; but I soon got bored with that. I guess I'm not a natural diary keeper, not like some people. Or maybe it's because nothing much interesting happens to me to be worth putting down.

The reason I'm writing an entry now is because it's a special time. Not a birthday or anything like that, more a different kind of anniversary altogether.

The thing is, it's exactly one year ago today that me and Mum and little Angeline first went to live in Scottley's. And what a time *that* was.

I don't think life will ever get that exciting again. Not really. I realise now that adventures like that are once-in-a-lifetime things. They don't happen everyday, more's the pity. Or maybe not. Perhaps I couldn't stand all the worrying.

Little Angeline isn't quite so little now, not any more. She's shot up like an electric car aerial these past few months and is quite a bit taller than a lot of other girls her age. But I'll probably always think of her as little Angeline, even if she ends up bigger than me in the end.

I'll probably always think of Mr Whiskers as Mr Whiskers too, even though he keeps on at me to call him Dad. (And Mum keeps on at him to shave his whiskers off, which is the one thing he *won't* do – not even for Mum. But I'm glad he doesn't. I don't think I'd like him so much, not without his whiskers; he wouldn't be so special.) Maybe I will start calling him Dad soon too. I know he's not my dad, not really. But he's the nearest thing I've got.

Yes, I guess that was maybe a bit of an exciting thing to happen, when Mum and Mr Whiskers got married. Mr Whiskers's mum came to the wedding to throw confetti at them and I was glad to see that she didn't have whiskers too. (Although his gran did a bit.)

We're pretty much settled in our new house too, the one we finally got in Western Drive. I was sure that we were going to be split up though; I was really terrified of that. I was quite convinced that Angeline and I would be taken into care and that Mum might be locked up somewhere for ever.

But it didn't come to that. Well, it couldn't really. Not when the managing director of Scottley's himself said how brave we were for tackling the burglars and stopping them getting away with his diamonds. And while he couldn't actually condone (which means 'approve of', apparently) us sneaking into his shop and living in Sports, Outdoors and Camping, he felt he just had to forgive us and to thank us for calling the police. Then he also added – just in case we put ideas into other people's heads – that a new security system had been installed, complete with twenty-four hour video-recording, and that anyone who tried to follow our example would be spotted and evicted immediately.

He also said, for the benefit of any would-be burglars, that a new, ultra-modern alarm system had been fitted too – and that included the door to the roof. Then he said that he wanted us to be dealt with leniently by the authorities in the circumstances and not to be punished too severely. So, maybe thanks to him, we didn't get sent into care at all, but we were put into a bed and breakfast for a week or so and then we moved into our house in Western Drive and we've been here ever since.

Oh yes, and then there was our reward.

The man who owns Scottley's (old Mr Scottley that is, not young Mr Scottley who is his son) wrote to us and asked if there was a small gift we might like to have from the store as a thank you present from him and as a souvenir. So we thought it over and we wrote back and told him about the ice cream sundaes we had helped ourselves to from Ice Cream Heaven and which we had never paid for. We explained that we'd meant to pay for them the next day by doing some cleaning, but we hadn't been able to because of the burglars. We said that those ice cream sundaes would be our present, if that was all right with him, and everything was square and we didn't owe him anything, and he didn't owe anything to us.

But then he wrote back and said that he didn't

feel one ice cream sundae each was enough, and that he wanted us to come to Scottley's and to have a free ice cream sundae once a month, every month for the rest of our lives! *The rest of our lives*!

Wow! I still can't believe that sometimes. Free ice cream sundaes until the day I die. I sometimes have to pinch myself to check that I'm not asleep and dreaming the whole thing.

She's been a lot different, Mum has, since we moved into our own house. She's sort of settled down a bit and she's been doing the same job for a whole six months too, which is quite a record for her. Six days was about her limit before.

Of course, she won't be able to do the job much longer. Not that she dislikes working part-time in Scottley's in Perfumes and Fragrances, she loves it. It's more because she's expecting the baby and she'll need to take some time off when it arrives.

I wonder if it'll be a boy or a girl. And if it is a boy, whether it'll have whiskers like Mr Whiskers, his dad.

Well, I'm sure we'll soon find out.

Anyway, I'd better go now, Mum's shouting at me to get a move on and she's starting to sound a bit impatient. She doesn't work today, it being her day off, but we're going into Scottley's anyway for our ice cream sundae. I think I'll have another Chocolate Cascade today. Just to remind me of our great adventure, which started exactly one year ago.

So that's it then. Better go. Mum's bellowing up the stairs like a herd of elephants and little (cross that out – *bigger*) Angeline is calling too. They want to go and get their ice creams.

I do wonder about one thing though, it's about Mum. She hasn't worried me for ages now and maybe she never will again. (Although I even worry about *not* worrying sometimes, I'm such a worrier.) But I do wonder about those itchy feet of hers and that gypsy in her soul.

Is he still there, that gypsy? Is he still there, deep down inside her? Maybe he's fast asleep somewhere. I think he is. I think he'll be asleep for a good long time now. But maybe one day, when we're all much older, he'll wake and stretch and yawn, and he'll be needing to wander again and to see new places. Maybe, maybe he will.

I don't think it's the end of it. Not by any means. You see, I know it's the end in some ways; but in other ways it's never the end at all and never will be. There is no end, not really, is there?

And in some ways, I don't want there to be.

Because I'll tell you my deepest secret, dear diary, that you're not ever to whisper to anyone else – I think I'm a little bit the same as Mum. I think I've got a touch of the gypsy in my soul too. For all that I'm a worrier, I'm a wanderer as well; I just need a home to come back to.

And I think that come the holidays, we'll all be off to see new places and see new things and to have extraordinary adventures, just like we always do. Because that's what Mum's like, really. Adventures come to her, just like friendly cats and dogs and pigeons wanting feeding.

Uh oh! They're calling for me again and they both sound really impatient now. I'd better go. I'll leave the rest for later. Better go and get a move on. Best get to Scottley's now for my ice cream sundae. From the best and greatest department store in the world.